the
gullah
mailman

the
gullah
mailman

Pierre McGowan

by Pierre McGowan

Illustrated by Nancy Ricker Rhett

Pentland Press, Inc.
England • USA • Scotland

PUBLISHED BY PENTLAND PRESS, INC.
5122 Bur Oak Circle, Raleigh, North Carolina 27612
United States of America
919-782-0281

ISBN 1-57197-199-8
Library of Congress Control Number: 99-75820

Printed in the United States of America

table of
contents

I am grateful to the following friends who provided me with valuable information for this book: Dennis Adams, Janette Alston, John Barton, Rusty Bishop, Clayton Boardman Jr., Ned Brown, Neils Christensen, Ralph Davis, Gam Foster, Kitty Harley, Margaret Hoffman, Lula Holmes, James H. Leach, Joseph "Crip" Legree, Ezekial Mack, Wilson McIntosh, Alexander Moore, Alyne Paysinger, Dr. Lawrence Rowland, William Scheper III, John Trask, Jr., and Henry Williams.

This book would not have been possible without the love, interest, and support of my daughter, Kelly McGowan-Scott.

And thanks to my wife Faye for her love, support and patience for the past two years while this effort was in progress.

Sam Doyle, Black Primitive Folk Artist

Two weeks before Mr. Doyle's death in 1985, I was near completion of the house my wife and I presently occupy, which is located on a small island off Seaside Road on St. Helena Island. In doing a general clean-up of the grounds adjacent to the house one day, I discovered that I had a pick-up truck load of old corrugated roofing tin and another load of scrap plywood that I needed to dispose of. The material was typical of what Mr. Doyle used for his work. I had known Sam Doyle for fifty years or so, during which time I leased some land from him for quail shooting. I wondered if I could make a deal with Sam for the two loads of material. He lived not far from us, so over I went. Sam was in his yard working, and I approached him with my proposition. I said, "Sam, you member de fus car my pa bin fuh use on he mail rout?"

"Yes, Suh," he said. "He stat wit a T Model Fode and den wen de A Model come out in '27 he switch to dat."

I said, "Sam, you sho rite. How ole you bin in '27?"

He said, "Bout 21 or so—I born in 1906." So Sam Doyle and I made our deal—a painting of my father in the Model T for two truckloads of material.

Two weeks went by and one morning in reading the *Beaufort Gazette*, I saw that Sam Doyle had died the previous day. I threw the paper down and went racing over to Sam's house in my truck. When I arrived, I was met with what to me was a ghastly sight. Normally in Sam's yard there were an estimated twenty-five to thirty-five pieces of his art. They would be leaning on trees, outbuildings, fences, or whatever—this is the way he advertised his wares. Well, there was not a single painting to be seen—all were gone. Standing near his house were three black ladies presumably discussing Sam's death. One of these ladies was Sam's niece, Janette Alston, who lived nearby. I approached and expressed my condolences regarding his passing. Then I asked what happened to all of the paintings, which had been in the yard waiting to be sold. Sam's niece replied, "Mr. John Tras Junya (John Trask, Jr.)—ob Orange Grove Plantashun, he cum by an carry all."

I asked, "Wa he do wittum?"

She said, "He carry all an puttem in de weyhouse (warehouse) for safekeep."

Then I said to Sam's niece, "You know Sam was spose to do a paintin fo me."

She said, "I know bout dat."

I replied, "Did Sam hab chance to do the ting fo me?"

She replied, "O, yes, Suh. He do um."

I asked, "Did Mr. Tras carry off my paintin?"

Sam's niece said, "O, no, Suh. He aint bin fo carry yo paintin—I got um fo yo."

I expressed my appreciation for her keeping the painting for me and told her I would pick it up the day following the funeral. Four days later I arrived at her house, and there was my painting leaning against a pine tree. Sam's niece came out of the house and I spoke first, saying, "You must a figa dis de day I bin fuh cum."

She said, "Yasah. I duz hab bof of dem paintins fo yo."

I said, "Bof—aint spose fo bin but wun."

She say, "Dats rite—but Sam do de fus wun an he aint lak um so he do um de secont time." The first version of his painting of my father is similar to the second, but without any wording on it. I gave her fifty dollars for rescuing them for me. They are believed to be the last paintings of Mr. Doyle before his death.

Until February of 1982, Sam Doyle was a virtually unknown Black Primitive Folk Artist. In 1980, the Corcoran Museum of Art (Washington, D.C.) undertook a study of this art form to determine to what extent Black Primitive Folk Art existed in the United States. Their study took them through thousands of miles of roads, mostly in the south, seeking an answer to this question. As a result of this exhaustive study, Sam Doyle became one of twenty artists selected to have their work presented in an exhibit at the Corcoran.

In February of 1982, John Trask Jr. of St. Helena Island bought an airline ticket for Sam Doyle to attend the exhibit in Washington, D.C. Sam had never been on an airplane before. Mr. Trask accompanied Sam to this exhibit and saw him safely home.

Prior to his artwork being recognized by the Corcoran, Sam could collect a fee of $25 to $50 for a piece of his work. By the time of his passing in 1985, the price for a Sam Doyle painting ranged from $150 to $400, depending on the complexity of the work. Since his death the price of a Sam Doyle piece has skyrocketed. One of his paintings today will bring $10,000 to $12,000—if you are lucky enough to find one.

Sam McGowan, circa 1887, Charleston, South Carolina

Sam McGowan was born in Abbeville, South Carolina, in the year of our Lord 1886. That was the year of the great South Carolina earthquake, and Sam liked to say that it took an earthquake to shake him loose and get him here. He was the grandson of Brigadier General Samuel McGowan, commanding general of the South Carolina Brigade CSA from January 1863 until the surrender of General Lee at Appomatox, Virginia, in April 1865. General McGowan later served as one of the three Associate Justices of the Supreme Court of South Carolina (1879–1893). Sam's mother, Clelia P. McGowan, was the first female to be elected to public office in South Carolina serving in Mayor Tom Stoney's administration in Charleston as Alderman. Sam loved to hunt, fish, and play around in general. His mother was a woman of means, and he was educated at Sewanee.

It was at Sewanee where Sam pulled off a most humorous practical joke. Practical jokes were his trademark. In those days (1903), attendance at church was mandatory. In good weather it was held outdoors. Everyone sat on wooden benches, including the choir, whose seats were elevated several feet higher than those of the congregation made up primarily of

Sam at age 35

Biltmore Forestry School, Brevard, NC Class of 1910 (Sam, inset)

students and faculty. At the site of this outdoor "chapel" where services were held, there was an open deep well complete with rope, pulley, bucket, and a dipper for the common use of all. Just before the choir arrived one Sunday morning, Sam drew a fresh bucket of water intended primarily for consumption by members of the choir. Into this tasty bucketful he secretly poured a sizeable dose of croton oil. Now croton oil is one of the most powerful, fast-acting laxatives known to man. The choir arrived, and most members stopped by the well for a refreshing drink. The choir was seated, and in about five minutes noticeable squirming was observed among the members. One by one those who had sipped the doctored water excused themselves and took off for the woods nearby gaining speed with every step.

Following Sewanee Sam took the one-year course (1910) at the first forestry school in the U.S. Dr. Carl A. Schenk founded this school in 1896

Dr. Carl A. Schenk, founder of Biltmore Forestry School, the first in the U.S.

in the mountains near Brevard, North Carolina. Dr. Schenk was attracted here by George Vanderbilt to manage the forests in and around the Biltmore House in Asheville, North Carolina. Dr. Schenk was from Germany and, according to Sam, he was the only man at the time to hold a Doctorate in Forestry—nothing but the best for George Vanderbilt. The school ran from 1896 to 1914, and at the outbreak of World War I, Dr. Schenk returned to Germany as his loyalties were with his native country. In 1963, the final reunion of the Biltmore Forestry School was held in Asheville, North Carolina. Among the attendees were Sam and Nancy McGowan.

Sam owned and operated a tire store in Akron, Ohio, and a shoe store in Augusta, Georgia, before being drafted into the U.S. Army in 1917. He was thirty-one years old and was sent to Fort Jackson, South Carolina, for basic training. As the only enlisted man at Fort Jackson with an automobile, he was in Columbia practically every night with his superior officers checking things out. That car managed to keep him at Fort Jackson until early November 1918, at which time he was sent to Newport News, Virginia, for embarkation to France. On November 11, 1918, he boarded a troop transport which was to sail at midnight. At about 8 P.M. an announcement was made that the war was over. He had beaten the rap. Sam said that his automobile probably saved his life.

In 1921, at the age of thirty-five, the most wonderful event ever to happen to my father occurred. He met my mother. She was a French lady by the name of Henriette Vurpillot from Mandeure, France, a small town in the French Alps located about ten miles from the Swiss border. She was sent by her family to Charleston to look after her ill uncle, who was the minister of the French Huguenot church on Meeting Street. She was twenty-five years old. In looking around for a place to live, she happened upon a lady who rented her a room at #3 St. Michael Place, which is in the S.O.B. section of Charleston. For the uninformed, S.O.B. means "South of Broad," and you are a nobody unless you live in this district. Beaufort native Tommy Jenkins, who has lived in Charleston County most of his life, says that Charleston is the only city in the U.S. where you receive thanks for calling someone an "S.O.B." My grandmother's house was #5 St. Michael's Place. Bingo. Once they met, and in spite of their age difference of ten years, it was love at first sight, and they were married in 1922 at my grandmother's summer cottage in Tryon, North Carolina. For whatever reason (no one knows), he affectionately began to call her Nancy and the name stuck.

In 1924, another meaningful event in Sam McGowan's life took place. He procured a job as rural mail carrier on St. Helena Island, South Carolina, at the little community then known as Frogmore. I believe it

Sam and Nancy's Sears Roebuck house constructed in 1924

impossible for a man to be better suited to a job than Sam McGowan was to this. It was perfect. It was like the answer to a prayer. Sam did not like anything resembling work, and he did not look at this endeavor as work. The mail route was strictly a one-man affair—thirty-seven miles long. He would arrive at the post office in Frogmore at 8 A.M., sort the mail for the route, and place it in neat stacks with a leather belt around each. By 9:30 A.M. he was off, completing the round by noon. He was home by 12:30, where he found lunch waiting on the table. After lunch came the biggest decision of the day—whether to go hunting or fishing.

After obtaining this "job," my parents wanted a house. Sam obtained a five-acre piece of land on the southern edge of St. Helena Island, located approximately half-way between Land's End and Coffin Point. St. Helena Island is twelve miles in length. On this property he built a Sears Roebuck pre-fabricated house. The house, according to Sam, had to face exactly due south in order to catch the prevailing breeze as air conditioning had not yet arrived. He had observed that the mansions on Bay Street in Beaufort were not parallel to the street, but faced due south. He concluded that the plantation owners who built these homes knew what they were doing. These Sears pre-fabs were prefabricated in the sense that every board was factory cut to its proper length, with each board having a number stamped on it which identified where it went. You received a set of construction drawings with a note saying that if you had the services of the right carpenter, you would not need to bring a saw to the job, everything was so precisely cut. The house was two stories high with a full basement. It came with a coal-fired furnace, and included hot water radiators in each room. This house was one of only three such heated houses on St. Helena Island. These Sears houses are now considered collector's items. In 1978, the house became the property of David and Linda Summerall. They have very tastefully restored the house and beautified the grounds to such an extent that it is periodically placed on the tour of homes. For seventy-five years the house has withstood all that Mother Nature has had to offer, enduring many powerful hurricanes without so much as a scratch. The house was shipped by rail to Port Royal where it was placed on a barge and then taken to the house site by water. Electricity came to St. Helena in 1937. From the day Sam built his house, he and my mother had electricity provided by a Delco system. This system provided only enough electricity for lighting through a system of batteries which were charged once a week by a small kerosene-driven generator.

Then came the children. To this union three sons were born—Sam, Jr., in 1924, Pierre in 1926, and Edward in 1928. From the time we learned to speak, our parents were called by their first names—Sam and Nancy. Located several miles out in front of the house were the barrier islands consisting from left to right facing south: Hunting, Fripp, Old, Pritchards, Capers, and Eddings or St. Phillips. It was on these uninhabited barrier islands and on the various creeks and rivers in between where the action could be found. Sam possessed all the necessary equipment and accessories such as boats, outboard motors, tents, and so on to make these islands readily accessible and comfortable upon arrival. We started accompanying our father on his weekend duck and deer-hunting forays when we reached the age of six. By the time we were ten or eleven, we were experienced enough to go on our own for Sam had taught us well. It was perfectly all right with our mother when we arrived home from school on Friday afternoon for us to jump into one of our boats accompanied by one of our black friends and our hunting dog and take off to one of the islands, not to be seen again until Sunday afternoon. She would not allow her boys to play football for Beaufort High School! One could get hurt doing that.

chapter 1

st. helena island

St. Helena Island is located in Beaufort County, South Carolina. The island is approximately twelve miles in length and two-and-one-half miles in width, and, generally speaking, runs east to west lengthwise. Its land area is approximately thirty square miles. It is bounded on the south by a string of barrier islands located about a mile out, which gives St. Helena's southern shoreline a bit of protection from the direct onslaught of waves from the Atlantic during hurricanes and from other storm systems approaching from southeasterly to southwesterly directions. It is bounded on the east by St. Helena Sound, on the west by Port Royal Sound, and on the north by three smaller islands namely Warsaw, Datha (now incorrectly named Dataw), and Polawanna.

During the past 400 years, St. Helena Island has witnessed its share of tragedy. Invasion, literally speaking, by the Spanish, French, and English, in the sixteenth and seventeenth centuries, and the taking of land from the various coastal Indian tribes, in my mind, has to rank near the top of the list in the conquest of one nation by another. Not only was the land taken from the Indians, but settlement of St. Helena and expansion by the English in the seventeenth century brought additional misery. Before the white man came to "America," there was little or no disease. From Europe came various diseases which the Indians contracted, killing them by the thousands. Further, many Indians were enslaved and were forced to move inland. By the end of the seventeenth century, many of the smaller Indian tribes had almost disappeared.[1]

It is, therefore, not surprising that in 1715 the dominant Indian tribe in the Port Royal area, the Yemassees, tired of seeing their land stolen, and retaliated with a vengeance. They began a war that lasted two years, and was called, appropriately, the Yemassee war. While most of the major fighting took place during this two-year period, the Yemassee continued to make raids on white settlements until 1728. In addition to the destruction of homes and other possessions, hundreds of white settlers were killed by Indians. The raising of cows and hogs was probably the

[1] Lawrence Rowland, Alexander Moore, and George C. Rogers, Jr. *The History of Beaufort County, South Carolina, Volume 1, 1514-1861*, South Carolina: University of South Carolina Press, 1996, p. 11.

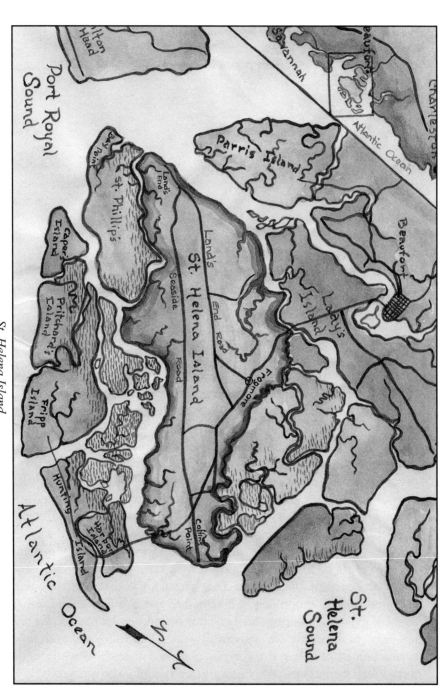

St. Helena Island

largest source of income to the English during this period. Unfortunately for the Indians, cattle raising required vast land areas. During the Yemassee uprising, thousands of cattle were also slain by the Indians. [2]

Hostilities were beginning to slow a bit with the Indians in 1730, but for the next forty years or so the English were kept extremely busy keeping the French and Spanish from making inroads into the Port Royal area. The most highly sought-after prize was Port Royal's deep harbor.[3]

During the 1740s, the growing of the blue-dye indigo was introduced to the region. By 1775, the largest single cash crop being grown and exported from the approximately forty plantations on St. Helena Island was indigo.[4]

The planting and growing of rice in the backwaters of South Carolina was occurring almost simultaneously with the raising of indigo, and these two endeavors required extensive manual labor. During most of the eighteenth century and in the nineteenth century up until the beginning of the Civil War, tens of thousands of slaves were dragged from their homes, primarily in Africa, and placed in bondage in this newly discovered continent. The planting of Sea Island Cotton on the islands in the Beaufort District near the end of the eighteenth century gave new impetus to the slave trade, since this was another labor-intensive crop.

St. Helena Island played no major significant military part during the Revolutionary War; however, at the war's end, all who were loyal to the British Crown left the district leaving their valuable property behind. The largest plantation on St. Helena Island—Frogmore—was left behind by Lieutenant Governor William Bull, Jr. Bull had remained a Tory throughout the revolution. A similar fate awaited all those in the thirteen colonies who sided with the British.[5]

The introduction of long staple or Sea Island cotton to the coastal region of South Carolina just prior to the turn of the nineteenth century turned many ordinary plantation owners into wealthy citizens. More specifically, St. Helena Island became one of the most productive cotton areas in South Carolina. Coffin Point and Frogmore Plantations, both located on St. Helena Island, became two of South Carolina's premier cotton plantations.[6] Of all the fortunes which were amassed from cotton production, all were done with slave labor. By the beginning of the Civil War in 1861, the principal crop grown on the approximately fifty plantations on St. Helena Island was cotton. The growing of cotton

[2] Ibid., 95-108.
[3] Ibid., 139-157.
[4] Ibid., 161-171.
[5] Roland, Moore, Rogers, I, 242.
[6] Ibid., 282-283.

required the extensive use of rich mud from nearby saltwater estuaries as a means of applying fertilizer. Also, in an effort to improve the soil, "dead" oyster shells from natural shell embankments along the riverbanks were brought in and scattered throughout the fields. This was the planter's means of "liming" the soil. While all of the rich Spartina grass mud has long since disappeared, one can walk through any recently plowed field on St. Helena Island after a rainfall and see thousands of pieces of white oyster shell. These pieces of shell give mute testimony to the slave labor required to place it there.

Wealth did not provide immunity from death at an early age on St. Helena. Diseases totally unknown to the medical community ran rampant, and the grim reaper carried off many who had not reached their tenth birthday. One has but to observe the dates of birth and death on many of the tombstones in the Fripp family graveyard, which is located on Seaside Road on St. Helena Island, to realize how common death was among the young. The white population of St. Helena Island probably did not exceed eighty families during the eighteenth and nineteenth centuries and was likened unto its own little community. Consequently, intermarriage between relatives was quite common. It is possible that this was also a contributing factor to the death of some at an early age.

For the first sixty years of the nineteenth century, life on St. Helena was for the most part uneventful. Cotton was king and plantations were expanded to increase production. In order to accomplish all of this, more labor was needed. It could come from only one source: Africa.

During the period from 1803–1808, forty thousand new slaves were transported to the South.[7] Big trouble was looming on the horizon over the matter of slavery, and after a decade of serious sparring with the North over this matter, it all came to a head on April 12, 1861, at Fort Sumter in Charleston Harbor.

On November 7, 1861, just six months following Fort Sumter, life on St. Helena Island became irrevocably changed for all of the plantation owners, their families, and their thousands of slaves. Admiral Samuel Dupont entered Port Royal Harbor with his massive Federal fleet, quickly knocking out the two small Confederate forts at the harbor's entrance. Within forty-eight hours after the first shot was fired there was not a white person remaining on St. Helena, and the slaves were left to their own devices. The abandonment of their plantations and slaves by the white owners gave rise to a bit of black folklore which was carried in the mind of at least one local resident until his death in 1985. On the rear of the dustjacket is a painting by noted Black Primitive Folk Artist Sam Doyle

[7] Ibid., 348.

entitled "Whooping Boy." This painting depicts a newly freed slave who has been decapitated and runs with his head tucked under his arm. The plantation owners, and their families left in such a hurry that most of their personal belongings were also left behind. It was on one such plantation that the story of "Whooping Boy" originated. The family silver was too heavy to take along, so the owner decided to bury it in an inconspicuous location. Taking along his most trusted slave to do the digging, the silver was buried. Once the silver was safely buried, the plantation owner then proceeded to kill his slave so that only the owner would know the silver's location. "Whooping Boy" is the slaves' ghost running around St. Helena Island whooping as he looks for his companions. Sam Doyle painted more than one version of "Whooping Boy."

Following on the heels of Admiral DuPont's invasion and complete Union takeover in the Beaufort District, which included all the outlying islands, came the horde of "missionaries." It was their feeling, or duty, to "raise" the black race. Most of these missionaries came with good intentions; however, some came to exploit the fallen South. With them came land speculators and carpetbaggers. No missionaries ever entered a foreign land more triumphantly or with a deeper sense of piety than did the curious wartime "missionaries" who swarmed into Beaufort and Port Royal.[8]

St. Helena Island became the birthplace of one of the first schools founded in the United States for the education of emancipated slaves. When the smoke cleared following the Battle of Port Royal Sound, the invading victorious Northern forces found themselves with 5,000 newly freed former slaves on St. Helena Island. In 1862, Penn School was founded by Laura Towne and Ellen Murray, two women who were supported by the Freedmen's Society in Philadelphia. Penn School operated as an independent school for African Americans continuously until 1948. Now known as Penn Center, its focus is primarily preservation of the Sea Island's history, culture, and environment. The center acts as a catalyst for the development of programs of self-sufficiency. The Penn School campus is designated as a National Historic Landmark district.

No district in any of the southern states lost more as a result of the Civil War than Beaufort County, South Carolina. It is ironic that the Secession movement began in Beaufort District. With the takeover of St. Helena and its neighboring islands early in the war, all was lost by abandonment. All real property was sold by the U.S. Tax Commission for

[8] Mason Crum, *Gullah*, North Carolina: Duke University Press, 1940, p.46.

nonpayment of taxes, with very little of the land later redeemed by the original owners at the cessation of hostilities.[9]

Most of the land on St. Helena Island was surveyed by federal surveyors and divided into ten-acre squares, with the lines running north–south and east–west. Curiously, some of the plantations, such as Ann Fripp Plantation, which lies immediately to the west of Edgar Fripp Plantation, was cut into sixty-foot-wide strips extending from the river on the south to Lands End Road on the north. These were called "wood" lots and provided the new owners—who were ex-slaves—with access to the river on the south and to two roads to the north. This system of land division provided the new owners with ample room for house construction and a ready wood supply for cooking, as well as for providing warmth in the winter. Many of the parcels of land either purchased or received as gift from the federal government by ex-slaves remain in the hands of their descendants even today.

From this distribution of land on St. Helena to ex-slaves immediately following the end of the Civil War, hundreds of mini-farms began to appear. When Sam McGowan arrived on St. Helena in 1924, he thought he had discovered the poorest section of the United States. If today's standard for measuring poverty had been used in 1924, then 99 percent of the black population and the majority of the white population would have fallen into the category of "living in poverty." The irony was that nobody living on St. Helena at this time ever considered themselves as poor. People were happy with what they had. No one went to bed hungry. The people looked out for each other. To be sure, no one was well off financially, but their mental outlook was incredible. In the forty years that Sam lived on St. Helena, I doubt that he ever heard of a single case of suicide within the black community.

In 1960 there was hardly a black family living on St. Helena Island that did not plant row crops to some extent, either for sale or for home consumption. Today it would be exceedingly difficult to find ten black families on St. Helena Island who till the soil for any purpose. With increased assistance from the federal and state governments it became easier to survive, and consequently labor-intensive endeavors such as planting became a thing of the past. Even the many large truck farms on the island that provided work for many began to find it difficult to secure their crops and had to look elsewhere. As late as 1960, the thousands of bushels of tomatoes which were harvested annually on St. Helena Island were all picked by black workers, most of whom resided on St. Helena. Today this work is all accomplished by migrant labor, mostly from

[9] Roland, Moore, Rogers, p.441.

Head of Family Land Certificate.

No. _473_

This Certifies, That on this _eleventh_ day of _May_ in the year of our Lord one thousand eight hundred and sixty-_four_ , the United States of America, by

Wm Henry Brisbane William E Wording & Dennis N Cooley

United States Direct Tax Commissioners for the District of South Carolina, under and by virtue of an act entitled "An act for the collection of Direct Taxes in Insurrectionary Districts within the United States, and for other purposes," approved June 7, 1862, and of the act amendatory of the same, approved February 6, 1863, and under and by virtue of the direction and instructions of the President of the United States issued to said Commissioners under date of September 16, 1863, for and in consideration of the sum of _Fifteen_

dollars, first paid by the purchaser hereinafter named, the receipt whereof is hereby acknowledged, doth hereby sell to _Demas Washington his heirs & assigns_ he being the head of a family and a colored citizen, the tract or parcel of land hereinafter set forth, and situate in the _Parish_ of _St Helena_ in the District of _Beaufort_ in the State of South Carolina, and described as follows, to wit:

_On St Helena Island.
Lot No Twelve (12) in Section Thirty-three (33)
Township One (1) South Range One (1) East containing
Ten (10) acres according to the United States survey
subject to public right of way._

to have and to hold the same, to h _im_ , h _is_ heirs and assigns, subject to all the provisions of the aforesaid acts.

Given under our hands, at _Beaufort_ , in the _Parish_ of _St Helena_ , in the District of _Beaufort_ and State aforesaid, on the day and in the year first above named

Wm Henry Brisbane
W E Wording
_____

U. S. Direct Tax Commissioners
for the District of South Carolina.

Head of Family Land Certificate wherein ex-slave Demas Washington purchased ten acres of land for $15 from the U.S. Direct Tax Commission

Mexico. Wages paid for this type of work were extremely low, and with construction booming at the local military bases and elsewhere within driving distance, the local black population simply moved away from menial, low-paying farm work.

Beginning in the mid-1930s, St. Helena Island began to lose many of its island-born sons and daughters to the lure of work in large northern cities. Some of these were close friends of mine that I hunted or played with in my youth. They spent their entire working lives "up North," returning only for brief family visits or for funerals. When their working days were over, many returned to St. Helena Island to live out their remaining days.

For me, growing up and living on St. Helena Island was simply wonderful. The segregation at the time sent me to all-white schools in nearby Beaufort, but I had more close black friends than white. It was a rare weekend-long trip "down the river" as we still call it, that did not include one of my black friends. Many times I have wished for the return of those delightful times.

chapter 2
the dialect: gullah

The importation of slaves from Africa and their intermingling with the white overseers and owners gave rise to an entirely new dialect— Gullah. When the slaves were first brought over, against their will, to the new continent, language was a major barrier. In many instances not only could the slaves not understand the white man, they could not understand each other. Slaves were taken from all over Africa, and consequently from many different tribes, each with its own dialect. They were mixed with each other in their placement, thereby compounding the language problem. What evolved over several hundred years is what some refer to as an abomination of the English language. Noted Charleston attorney and avid student of Gullah, Alfred "Fritz" Von Kolnitz, in his book *Cryin' in de Wilderness*, which he published in 1937, states that the Lowcountry (of South Carolina) is the birthplace and home of that strangely twisted form of the English language known as Gullah. He states that Gullah is that violation of the English language which has resulted from the efforts of original African savages and their immediate offspring, to compromise their native tongues with the already idiomized form of English used by coastal South Carolinians. Von Kolnitz states further that Gullah is a pleasing, quite soft, but somewhat guttural dialect which represents the Lowcountry Negro's attempt to speak our language, but which lapses in its most primitive stages into an actual admixture of native African roots and phrases.[1]

Is the origin of Gullah African or English? According to Mason Crum in his book *Gullah*, the answer is definitive: it is almost wholly English of the seventeenth and eighteenth centuries, with perhaps a score of African words remaining. Very early, the slaves picked up the dialect of the illiterate indentured servants of the colonies, the "uneducated English." It may be said that while the body of the dialect is English, its spirit is African.[2]

---

[1] Alfred "Fritz" von Kolnitz, *Cryin' in de Wilderness*, Charleston, S.C.: Walker, Evans, and Cogswell, 1937, pp. 5-6.
[2] Crum, p.111.

Regarding the origin of the term Gullah, Mason Crum stated that the origin of the word is almost certainly a corruption of the African Gola or Gora, names of African tribes living in Liberia, east of the city of Morovia. For a long time, Gullah was considered a modification of the African Angola, but this belief is barely tenable now.[3]

There are other factors which affected the Gullah dialect besides the influence of the English peasant and the indentured servant of the Royal government. First, there was the influence from plantation life in the West Indies from which the first slaves came to the Carolina coast.[4] The first slaves in South Carolina were brought over by Sir John Yeamans from Barbados Island in 1677 for his Ashley River plantation.[5] Later, slaves came directly from Africa, but many were shipped from the sugar islands, seasoned workmen who had already picked up a modicum of language from the rich plantation barons of Barbados and Jamaica.[6] It has also been suggested that an important factor in the development of Gullah was the "baby talk" or abbreviated English used by overseers in directing the new slaves who knew no English. In this simplified speech, tenses, genders, and numbers were reduced, and only a minimum of language remained to convey simple instructions, a device often used in communication with foreigners.[7] Doubtless another factor in the development of Gullah was the simple language concepts of the unseasoned slaves who came fresh from the barracoons of Senegal and Sierra Leone with their simple dialects, to meet the language of the white man in Carolina. The Negro's first impulse was to cut his speech down, use as little of it as possible, take every shortcut available, and acquire just enough to meet his elemental needs. In the process, he made a perfect wreck of English, violating every rule of grammar, caring only to be understood; and while in the language of the street he "murdered the King's English," his meaning was always unmistakable. In the process, he wrought out some of the most homely and at the same time piquant idioms in the language.[8]

Alfred von Kolnitz records for posterity a bit of Gullah and logic which took place in a conversation with a black man during the depression in the mid-1930s. He was driving along a country road in a remote section of the Carolina Lowcountry when he happened upon this man plowing behind an ox. He stopped to chat with him and inquired into what he was planting. "Mekkin up dis lan fuh plant corn Suh," he said.

[3] Ibid., preface.
[4] Ibid., p112.
[5] Ibid., p112.
[6] Ibid., p112.
[7] Ibid., p113.
[8] Ibid., p113.

"You are about the last person left around here, aren't you?" von Kolnitz asked.

The man replied, "Yes, Suh, me an fo head ob gran (grandchildren). De res bin gone to de city fuh scape de presshun."

"Aren't you afraid of the depression, too?" von Kolnitz inquired.

This old man straightened his shoulders bent by years of toil, threw his head back proudly and said, "Young massa, dat presshun new-come; I bin hyuh. New come can't beat bin hyuh."

The most prolific and in many respects the greatest of all the writers of Gullah dialect was the late Ambrose Elliot Gonzales of Columbia.[9] Mr. Gonzales' father was born in Cuba and came to this country as a refugee. He married an Elliot of an aristocratic rice-growing family with holdings on the Combahee River. It was here where the young Ambrose Gonzales was introduced to Gullah. Mr. Gonzales was born in 1857 and died in 1926. In 1891, he and his brother, N. G. Gonzales, founded *The State* newspaper in Columbia, South Carolina. Ambrose Gonzales was its editor. In addition to hundreds of articles on Gullah which he wrote and published in his own newspaper, he wrote and published the following books: *The Black Border, With Aesop Along the Black Border, The Captain-Stories of the Black Border,* and *Laguerre, A Gascon of the Black Border.* In my opinion these books are written in the purest of Gullah. Roughly speaking, what I consider to be pure Gullah was that found along the coast of South Carolina from Georgetown as its northernmost extremity, south to the site of the rice plantations on the Altamaha River near Brunswick, Georgia, and extending inland from the coast approximately twenty miles. Having been raised on St. Helena Island from infancy and growing up very close to a black family with nine children, I became well acquainted with Gullah early in life. The ratio of blacks to whites on St. Helena Island during the first half of this century was approximately fifty to one, and in order to survive, learning to speak Gullah was a necessity. In Sam's thirty-one years on the mail route, his job was made easier by the fact that he knew and could speak the dialect when he arrived in 1924 (having been raised in Charleston). Approximately 95 percent of his constituents on his mail route spoke only Gullah.

It can be said that the Gullah dialect is one of "short cuts" taken to the limit. Following are some examples of this extremism.

the	de
they	dey
think	tink

[9] Ibid., p110.

that	dat
this	dis
them	dem
there	dey
those	dose

Generally, on words that have the consonant "r" as the third letter in the word, the word is almost invariably altered. For example:

turn	tun
bird	bud
yard	yad
farm	fam
for	fuh
card	cad
burn	bun

Words that end in the consonant "r" are generally changed also.

never	nebba
other	odda

Words that end in "th" also took a hit.

Smith	Smit
both	bof
south	sout
with	wit

Words that begin with "wh" are likewise changed.

where	wey
what	wa
when	wen

Samples of other newly created words are:

little   le
(little bird = le bud)
going   gwine
(I'm going to Church. = Ise gwine to Chuch.)
Aren't you   enty
(Aren't you going to work? = Enty hunnah gwine fuh wuk?)

The attack on English was endless. Contractions without benefit of an apostrophe ruled supreme. One of the most commonly used words in this new dialect was the word "shum." The root of this word is "see," and when used behind any pronoun has unlimited possibilities.

You shum?
[Did you see (any person or group, male or female, or object(s)?]
I shum.
(I see.)

These are but a few examples of the hundreds of words that evolved.

One of the peculiarities of Gullah lies in the fact that it has some words that sound almost alike, so much so that the unattuned ear finds them unintelligible. For instance the word "dey" can mean "they," "there is" and "are" plus the double use meaning "is there" or "are there." It may also mean deer. As one plantation guide allegedly told a northern hunter who grew tired of waiting on a deer on a hunting stand and suggested moving: "Dey ain't no use fuh move. When you dey, de dey ain't dey dey and when de dey dey dey, you ain't dey dey."[10] Translation is: "There is no point in moving. When you are there, the deer are not there, and when the deer are there you are not there."

Gullah has no respect for tense, number, or gender. A man's wife is often referred to as "him" or even "it." When pure Gullah is spoken, the conversation is very fast moving, not unlike a staccato or bursts from a machine gun. There is an ancient anonymous Latin saying that "necessity is the mother of invention." This quote could hardly be truer regarding the evolution of the Gullah dialect.

Unfortunately, pure Gullah as I knew it is on its way out. It will forever remain in print and on recordings, but the passing of the present generation will leave behind only a shadow of the original dialect. In an article written by Jack Leland, staff writer for the *Charleston Evening Post*, which was published in the *Post* on August 8, 1974, he correctly predicted the demise of Gullah. He listed the following as factors contributing to its death: public schooling, mobility, and the predilection of church ministry and various black organization leaders to point at the dialect with scorn and to urge its abandonment.

[10] Jack Leland. "A Fast Disappearing Lowcountry Dialect," *Charleston Evening Post*, 8 August 1974, p. 5.

chapter 3

the mailman's wife

Henriette (Nancy) Vurpillot shortly after her arrival in Charleston, SC in 1921

When Marie Henriette Vurpillot arrived at #3 St. Michael, Charleston, South Carolina, in 1921, she was totally unaware, of course, that her life would be forever changed. Her original plans were to remain in Charleston, possibly for two to three months, during which time she would hopefully nurse her uncle back to good health. Sam McGowan changed all of this. Upon her uncle's recovery, Nancy returned to her native France for a short visit, returning in the summer of 1922. Immediately upon her return, she and Sam were married in a quiet family wedding at Sam's mother's summer cottage in Tryon, North Carolina. In 1931, she boarded an ocean liner in New York City accompanied by her three very active young sons for a year-long visit to Mandeure, France. While in France, Beau Sam and I attended elementary school. When Sam met us at the train station in Yemassee after a year in France, not a word of English was spoken by us. Nancy made several more trips to France in later years, but these were of much shorter duration and she traveled alone.

Living in a remote section on St. Helena Island for forty-two years would bring out the best in any woman who possesses special qualities, I suspect. And did she have special qualities. Having spent the first twenty-five years of her life on a farm in France did not hurt either. She was a loving wife and mother, doctor, nurse, advisor, and an excellent cook. There were many Beaufort and St. Helena Island residents who, once having sat at her table, wished for a return invitation.

A Near Fatal Accident

In 1925, Sam bought my mother her own Model T Ford. In 1927, Nancy, accompanied by three close friends, was on her way to a shopping trip in Savannah. This was an all-day long affair, as one had to drive by way of Gardens Corner and then on U.S. 17 to Savannah. As Nancy approached the railroad crossing at Sheldon (there was no viaduct over the railroad crossing back then), a freight train darted across in front of the car. In order to avoid a collision with the train, she pulled the steering wheel hard to the right. The Model T turned completely over, landing on its back. All of the car's occupants (including Nancy) suffered broken bones as well as various cuts and bruises. This accident had such a profound effect on Nancy that she never got behind the steering wheel of an automobile again during the remainder of her life.

The Bottle

It was an extremely rare occasion that Nancy visited the Frogmore Post Office. She was from the old country and therefore a homebody, and she loved her home so much that she found things there to occupy her time. She was compelled, however, by her citizenship status to make a visit to the post office every January, like it or not. For, you see, Nancy came to this country as an alien in 1921; and when she died sixty-six years later, she was still an alien, having never become a naturalized American. By law she was required to register as an alien at a United States Post Office each January. On one such visit to the post office in January 1940, she noticed a black woman with whom she was casually acquainted wearing a large bandage around her left thumb. She asked the woman if she would mind removing the bandage in order that my mother might take a look at the problem. The condition of the bandage itself was what attracted Nancy's attention. The bandage was removed and Nancy was aghast at what she saw. The thumb was swollen to twice its original

Taken from SS City of Savannah after its foundering in the hurricane of 1893. Background: Nancy talks to lady with infected thumb.

size and was horribly infected. The woman explained that she had accidentally broken off the barb from the head of a shrimp under the skin and that she had been unable to extract it. Nancy made her own diagnosis—blood poisoning—and knew that this woman's life was in immediate danger. Nancy made Sam stop his work instantly and take the woman to Doctor William Ryan's office in Beaufort. Dr. Ryan's diagnosis confirmed Nancy's opinion, and he was required to remove part of the thumb in order to stop the infection from spreading and prevent blood poisoning.

The thumb healed satisfactorily and two months later, the woman sent a message to Nancy requesting that Nancy pay her a visit. Several days after receiving this message, Sam took Nancy to see the woman. It was during this visit that the woman gave Nancy a bottle that her father-in-law had salvaged from the steamship *City of Savannah*. The *City of Savannah* was caught off the coast of South Carolina during the 1893 hurricane, which was probably the most devastating storm ever to strike the eastern seaboard of the United States. This ship was driven ashore about three miles off the southern end of Hunting Island. She was a wooden ship carrying a cargo of leather goods—primarily shoes. The hull of the ship did not break apart for several weeks following its grounding, thereby affording ample time for salvage operations to take place. Salvage typically consisted of ex-slaves and their family members rowing out to the wreck in wooden homemade *bateaux*, tying their craft alongside, and diving into the submerged holds to retrieve the booty. Sam said that this operation continued for several weeks and ended only when one of the divers failed to return. It was on one such trip that the woman's father-in-law returned home with a pair of beautiful porcelain bottles. They were retrieved from the pilothouse on the ship and were used to contain water. From a lip that protrudes about one-half inch outward at the widest part of the bottle, it is obvious that each sat in a gimbal. This enabled the bottle to remain upright when the ship rolled from side to side. The bottle has a beautiful rope design around its circumference at seven locations and also has the company coat of arms on it. The company that owned the steamship *City of Savannah* was the Ocean Steamship Company.

Nancy's Only Hunt

There is one thing that Nancy did not involve herself with and that was hunting. She was never known to handle a firearm of any description during her entire life. During the fall of 1937, Bill Dorman of Princeton, New Jersey, who was the owner of Fripp Island and a close friend of Sam

Nancy McGowan on her first and only deer hunt

and Nancy, got in touch with Sam and asked him to organize a deer hunt. Sam made the necessary arrangements, and upon learning that Bill Dorman's wife was coming along, he asked Nancy to attend to keep Mrs. Dorman company. So Nancy, unlike Mrs. Dorman, went along, but not to hunt. This hunt was typical for the time with "standers," as it were, posted at various locations around the island with the deer being moved about by dogs accompanied by "drivers." Sam placed Mrs. Dorman on the most renowned stand on Fripp Island, approximately where the tennis courts are presently located. Due to the geographical configuration of Fripp Island, this narrow strip of land was appropriately called "The Narrows" (with the ocean on the south and the marsh on the north). Mrs. Dorman's shotgun was a twenty-gauge double loaded with number three buckshot. Nancy brought along a book to pass the time with and walked through the woods to the beach. Fripp Island was considerably wider in 1937 and was virtually a jungle. Her distance from Mrs. Dorman was approximately two-hundred-and-fifty yards. She sat on a palmetto log and began reading her book, listening to the dog's voices in the distance. About a half an hour after Nancy sat down and started reading, she became conscious of something staring at her. She looked up and standing hardly ten yards from her was an eight point buck. For what seemed like a full minute, they stared at each other, each seemingly knowing that no danger was present. Finally this beautiful animal turned north and unhurriedly walked directly toward Mrs. Dorman's stand. In approximately two minutes Nancy heard sharp cracks from that little twenty-gauge shotgun. Mrs. Dorman was deadly with it, and she did not miss. When Bill Dorman and Sam saw how distraught Nancy was after looking at her deer lying dead on the ground, the hunt was brought to an immediate end. Nancy never went hunting again even as a spectator.

Clover

The Clover Club of Beaufort is unquestionably one of the most unique and long lasting clubs in the United States. It was founded in 1891 in Beaufort as a music and literary organization. It was the brainchild of Mary Elizabeth Waterhouse, and it is primarily due to this organization that the citizens of Beaufort County have such a beautiful library today. The membership established from its inception was limited to thirty and that number remains.

Only death, permanent departure of a member, or retirement due to age can create an opening for membership. Being well acquainted with this organization for many years as the result of Nancy's long membership, it has been my perception that to be extended an invitation to become a member of Clover is akin to receiving an invitation for an audience with the Pope.

Each lady is required to give a "paper" on an assigned topic on a specific date each year. Similarly, each lady must host one meeting each year in her home. Fortunately, a "paper" presentation for a particular member will not fall on the same date as her turn to be hostess. Regular meetings of Clover begin on the second Monday in October and continue into May. The annual meeting is held on the second Monday in March each year for the purpose of hearing committee reports and receiving "paper" and hostess assignments for the following year.

Clover's motto, which was penned in 1891, is "For The Best That Thou Canst Be, Is The Service Asked Of Thee."

Nancy McGowan was inducted into the Clover Club in March 1938, and I do not believe there was a member who took on this responsibility more seriously than she. There is an old saying that "Hell hath no fury like a woman scorned." In the case of the McGowan household, this saying could be altered to read "Hell hath no fury like a woman preparing her Clover Paper or preparing her home as Clover Hostess." When Nancy was working on her annual Clover Paper, Sam and the boys simply disappeared. And on the one day during the year when it was her turn to be hostess, the male McGowans stayed away in droves. At the end of that fateful day when the last guest drove out of the yard, all became peaceful and serene once again.

Clover remains very active today and is a vital part of the Beaufort scene. The membership still numbers thirty and will probably always remain so.

Butterfly Strips

There are many learned folk who believe that so-called butterfly strips are a fairly recent invention. Not so. Butterfly strips are used with regularity in the modern medical field for closing wounds and are a substitute for stitches. I believe that this method is used in certain instances in order to reduce the size of the scar.

On New Year's Eve in 1939, my younger brother Ed and I departed just after dark on a trout gigging trip. We had planned on being home by midnight or so. Sam and Nancy had made plans to attend a New Year's Eve party from which they were also expected home shortly after midnight. Ed and I knew the waters within five miles of our house in any direction extremely well in daylight or darkness, and by eight o'clock we were at our intended destination—the intersection of Club Bridge Creek, Trenchards Inlet and the eastern end of Station Creek. We were in a twelve-foot *bateau* with our propulsion provided by a three-horsepower Bendix Eclipse air-cooled outboard motor. Shortly after arriving, we ignited our gasoline torch and began gigging. The air temperature was slightly below freezing and the water temperature was in the vicinity of fifty degrees Fahrenheit. After a few moment's travel along the extreme northeastern shoreline of Trenchards Inlet, we discovered a very large school of trout. I began gigging and had dropped about thirty trout into the boat when I lost my balance and fell overboard backward. When I started falling, I immediately dropped the gig and threw my hands behind me to break the fall. My feet remained inside the boat, and the water being only about a foot in depth, I managed to keep most of my body dry. Ed helped me back into the boat and I immediately went back to gigging. At the time the only damage I thought had occurred was to my pride and wet posterior. In the darkness and extremely cold temperature I was not aware of the damage which had occurred to my left wrist.

After about five minutes had elapsed and another dozen or so trout in the boat, I felt the wooden handle of the gig becoming sticky. I held the gig down near the water's edge under the light which was designed to reflect downward, and gasped at what I saw. We were gigging along the shoreline among tall clusters of oysters; and when I fell, my wrist obviously had landed on one of these. Directly behind my thumb, at the wrist, was a smooth incision two-inches long and approximately a quarter-of-an-inch deep. The wound was open and was also about a quarter-of-an-inch wide. At each heartbeat blood was pumping out, so I knew I had an opening in an artery. We took a pocketknife and tore a strip out of one of my trouser legs to fashion a tourniquet, using the knife as a twisting instrument. We then cranked that little outboard and headed home, arriving about 1 A.M. When Sam and Nancy arrived home from their New Year's Eve party a few minutes later, I was at the kitchen sink washing my wound. Blood was all over the kitchen, and Nancy almost fainted when she walked into the room. She took a good look at my wound and simply said, "This will not wait until tomorrow; we are going to Margaret's house now." Off we went at 1:30 in the morning on New Year's Day, 1940, to get Margaret Sanders out of bed. There was a road connecting our house with hers, and the distance was approximately one-quarter mile. Margaret Sanders was a registered nurse, although she had not practiced her profession in many years. She looked at the wound and decided that under the circumstances she would tackle the job herself. First, she poured about half a bottle of iodine on the wound, warning me beforehand that this was going to burn like crazy. She was right on target. Then, after removing the excess iodine and blood, she started at one end of the wound and began closing it with tiny strips of adhesive tape she had cut from a large roll. It took her about twelve of the tiny strips to complete the job, and then she wrapped my entire wrist in a gauze bandage. Then she fashioned a splint using a piece of flat wood from a tomato crate and wrapped it with gauze to stabilize the wrist and keep me from reopening the wound. Two days later she removed the splint and outer bandage for inspection. There was no sign of infection, and the wound was healing very nicely. She replaced the bandage and splint. About a week later when she removed everything, including her "butterfly strips," she told me I was well enough to bring her a mess of trout.

chapter 4

the early years

The Roads on St. Helena

When my parents arrived on St. Helena Island in 1924, it was a dream come true for them. Peace and tranquility reigned. The population of St. Helena consisted of approximately five thousand blacks who were all descendants of slaves and sixty-five whites. Construction on the bridge connecting Lady's Island and Beaufort did not begin until 1925 with completion coming in early 1927. There were perhaps a dozen automobiles on St. Helena along with a few farm trucks. There were no paved roads, and most of the roads consisted of two deep ruts. The road from the Chapel of Ease to Frogmore and then to Lady's Island were covered with oyster shell for stability. After several year's use with the oyster shell topping, these roads developed a corrugated or "washboard" surface, and the only way to drive them without shaking the car and its occupants to pieces was to drive at five miles per hour or at thirty-five miles per hour. The men usually drove at the latter speed. This way you hit every other corrugation and the ride was fairly smooth until you slowed down. One day this corrugated effect provided an unexpected but delightful surprise. We were on the school bus headed home after school one afternoon when we fell in behind a truck belonging to the Old Fort Packing Company of Walterboro, South Carolina, a meatpacking firm. We were quick to notice that the rear door of the truck had become unlatched and that a large box was inching closer to the door as the truck bounced along. After about a mile of this, the box fell out and landed in the middle of the road. Our driver, Mr. Bishop (Big Bish as he was affectionately known), came to a halt and let us retrieve the box. It was a fifty-pound box of pork spare ribs. Needless to say, everyone on the bus, including Big Bish, took home a slab of spare ribs.

It took a good bit of experience to drive those deep rut dirt roads, especially stopping and then starting again without spinning the wheels in the sand and bogging the rear of the car down to the axle. When this happened you had to find someone nearby with a pair of oxen. High speed driving on dirt roads was something else again. By 1934, Sam had become very experienced in this endeavor, having had about ten years on

Miss Rossa Cooley (l) and Miss Grace House, 1920. Miss Cooley was the principal at Penn School from 1904-1944. She was a graduate of Vassar. Miss House was Assistant Principal during the same period. She was a graduate of Columbia Teachers College in New York. The photograph was taken one half mile east of "old" Frogmore and this road is now US 21.

Frogmore General Store and Post Office, circa 1920. This structure now houses the Red Piano Too Art Gallery. Note the oyster shell topping on the road surface.

Road running through Penn School toward the Chapel of Ease, circa 1920. Roadway is topped with oyster shell.

the mail route. In 1934, I was eight years old, and I remember going with Sam on a Saturday afternoon to visit a friend at Coffin Point. While we were there, he took several pops before we headed home. He had just purchased a new 1934 Ford V-8, the second one on the Island—Miss Cooley, the Grand Dame at Penn School, bought the first one—and when we reached a point on Seaside Road about where Worthington's Store was located (now Russel's Roadhouse Restaurant), he said, "Son, let me show you how to drive these dirt roads." In those days, this was a powerful machine with its eighty-five horses. He gave it a little juice, turning the steering wheel to the right and putting the left wheels of the car on the mound of earth between the ruts. He then stepped the speed up to about forty miles per hour. Seaside Road is, for all practical purposes, as straight as an arrow and down it we went at this speed trailing a huge cloud of dust the likes of which had never been seen before. I was a bit frightened, but Sam never came close to losing control of the car. Those dirt roads were his toy. Sam blamed this little incident on the two nips he took at Coffin Point.

During extremely bad road conditions when the use of an automobile was impossible, my father had a black friend living near Frogmore who had a horse and buggy he could rent. The route on days like this would become an all-day affair. In thirty-one years on the mail route, he resorted to this mode of transportation only three times.

Maybe St. Helena's First Accident

In thirty-one years on the mail route, the only accident my father had was with a large billy goat. Back then a section of his route carried him down Dulamo Road, then west on a narrow crossover road which then proceeded through what is now the Henry Farm. While on the narrow portion of the road one day, he rounded a curve and there stood a large billy goat. Both sides of the road were heavily wooded, and the goat had no place to go except to try and outrun the Model A bearing down on him. The goat was doing well when my father speeded up a bit to see how fast the goat could really go. After a few seconds at the increased speed, the goat made an about face and charged the monster. Just before its impact with the front bumper, my father had nearly gotten his machine to a stop. A terrific collision ensued after which my father got out of his car and walked around to the front to examine the goat. The goat was knocked unconscious by the blow, and my father thought he was dead. After a wait of about a minute, the goat got to his feet, shook his head, and took a look at his adversary. He then took off down the road, this time never looking back.

The Little Black Book

Now, Sam might have possessed some faults as we are all prone to have, but no one could say that his intelligence was lacking. His car, while on the mail route, was akin to a traveling post office. Most of the island's inhabitants did not have the means to get to the post office at Frogmore on a moment's notice, so they relied on my father to look out for them, particularly when it came to postal matters. He sold stamps and money orders right out of the car window. For packages, he would accept the package, throw it in the back seat, take the sender's two dollars, weigh the package when he got back to the post office, and return the proper change the next day. This procedure continued for the entire thirty-one years he carried the mail. In 1924, after about six months on the job, it occurred to him that there were no records kept of these transactions. He obtained a little black notebook, and at the beginning of each day he would enter the cash received from the postmistress, the number of stamps in each denomination, and so on. Along the route he would enter all transactions made, and upon returning to the post office he would turn over to the postmistress all cash, unsold stamps, and money order receipts, all of which were dutifully entered into his notebook. Then he would have the postmistress initial each day's transactions. This procedure went on for several years, and then one morning at about nine o'clock there was a knock on the post office door. The door was opened and there stood two gentlemen wearing full dress suits, both carrying briefcases and presenting badges—United States Postal Inspectors. It took several days for them to complete their audit, and upon its completion the postmistress was sent to the penitentiary for embezzlement. One of the postal inspectors later told my father that were it not for his little notebook, he would have cooled his heels in Atlanta for a spell.

chapter 5
on the mail route

Wife's Instructions

Many things happened to my father during his thirty-one years on the mail route, some very humorous. When he came across a package that was too large to leave in the mailbox at the side of the road, he would deliver it to the recipient's house. One day he delivered a package to the front door of one of St. Helena's leading citizens. No one was home so he left the package on the doorstep. It was hard for him not to notice a note held by a thumbtack on the door. The note which was obviously written by the wife to the husband read, "Fix your own damn lunch."

Reading the Mail

I don't think my father passed up too many opportunities to peruse personal information written on postcards he was delivering, especially if the recipient was a close friend. A lady who lived on St. Helena Island most of her life told me she met my father at the mailbox one day, and as he handed her the mail he said, "I see your sister in North Carolina wants you to send her some money."

Oyster Barter

My parents loved to eat the local oysters which were so bountiful. My mother made the most wonderful oyster stew, and it was regular fare for the table during the cold months of the year. Sam struck a deal with a black friend who knew where to get the best oysters. For the first twenty years of Sam's carrying the mail on St. Helena, every Friday during the winter while on his route he opened his friend's mail box whether there was any mail for him or not. Inside would be a quart of the most beautiful shucked oysters. My father would remove the oysters from the mailbox, and in its place would leave twenty-five cents and an empty jar. During the last eleven years of Sam's carrying the mail, the price per quart rose to fifty cents. Inflation had come to St. Helena.

Oyster delivery by U.S. mail

Whiskey Delivery by U.S. Mail

One day while on his route, this woman met my father with a package that needed to be mailed to her son in Philadelphia. He threw the package on the seat in the rear, took her money, and told her he would return her change the next day. Most of the moonshine whiskey made on St. Helena Island had an awful, very distinct odor. When he got about a fourth of a mile down the road, the smell hit him. She was mailing two one-half gallon fruit jars of moonshine to her son, and one of the jars had broken when he threw the package on the back seat. He turned around and went back to the house where he picked up the package, only this time he pulled into her yard. When she saw him coming, she thought she'd be going to jail for she knew it was against the law to ship whiskey by mail, much less illicit whiskey. She went into what they call on St. Helena "de histerics," for she thought my father would take her in right then. She calmed down only when Sam assured her there would be no reporting of the incident—no jail time, no fine—only an admonishment from my father never to try it again. For you see, he hunted quail on her land. Prior to the occurrence of this incident, Sam had probably mailed moonshine whiskey many times.

Rattlesnake

One summer day about two miles before reaching Worthington, or Wards store, as it was called, Sam killed a very large rattlesnake he spotted crossing Seaside Road, a fairly common occurrence back then. He knew there would be a number of people at the store from the Coffin Point area waiting to see if there was any mail for them. Sam was always ready to put a little humor into what was a dull day, so he coiled the dead rattlesnake behind the driver's seat with its head in position as though it was ready to strike. A few minutes later he pulled into Wards store where as he suspected, a good crowd was waiting. He carried the community mail into the store, picked out a youngster about twelve years old, and instructed him to go out to his car, open the door on the driver's side, pull back the seat, and bring in a "package" lying on the floor. In the meantime Sam had alerted Mr. Worthington and the others in the store what he was up to. Everything went as planned, and when the youngster reached behind the seat to retrieve the "package," there was a split second of hesitation on his part. He recoiled instantly, hitting his head on the door jamb. When he regained his senses, he was last seen hauling it down Seaside Road, followed by a cloud of dust while his audience roared with laughter.

The Grumman Wildcat

One afternoon in the summer of 1942, I was sitting in a barbershop on Bay Street in Beaufort when a huge Marine Corps truck came by with a Grumman Wildcat fighter plane which had flown from Page Field on Parris Island on it. There were six squadrons of these planes stationed there during the early part of World War II. I noticed that it had obviously made a wheels-up landing somewhere, since all three propeller blades were bent backward and the engine cowling was filled with dirt and grass. Several hours later when I got home, I thought I had an interesting story to tell my parents about seeing that airplane. Sam had a much more interesting story to tell about the same airplane. He was on his mail route traveling east on Seaside Road in the vicinity of the Station Creek Landing when he saw the Grumman coming. It was about fifty feet off the ground coming straight for him about a hundred yards away. Instinct told him the plane was crippled and was about to make a crash landing. Just before the plane reached him, the young pilot had just enough speed left to pull up and avoid colliding with his car. Immediately after passing over his car, the plane made a belly landing in an open field. Sam stopped and went over to the airplane where he congratulated the pilot for making such a fine dead-stick landing.

Chage Um to My Pa

When I was about ten years old, accompanied by two of my young black friends, I walked over to Manny William's store at Club Bridge Creek one Saturday morning. This was a distance of about one mile from our house. In those days you could purchase a fair-sized Baby Ruth candy bar for a penny. I had no money whatsoever, but I picked up six of the candy bars and told Manny to "chage um to my pa." In other words, collect the six cents from him when he came around on his mail route later that morning.

I shared the candy with my friends and went home. No more thoughts entered my mind about this supposedly innocent little caper until my father came home. He sought me out immediately and inquired about the candy bar charge at Manny William's store. I told him I was the guilty party. Now my father gave me only two whippings with his belt during my entire youth; this one was the first and it was a dandy, procuring the desired results. It put an immediate end to "chaging" at Manny William's store, or to any other store for that matter. Sam was very close with a dollar, and during his lifetime he never bought a thing he could not pay for in cash.

"Oooh damn!"

chapter 6
fishing

(l-r) Sam, Ed, and Pierre upon returning from a fishing trip with their father in April, 1937. Sam Sr. caught the fish.

Drum Fishing

Drum fishing with a handline is about as exciting as watching a glacier move. It is a sport that evolved in this country long before the Civil War. It involves going out into the vast expanses of Port Royal or St. Helena Sound, anchoring your *bateau* over your favorite "drop," and waiting hours on end for these fickle fish to bite.

Drum fish are large (average sixty pounds) bottom feeders. Their flesh is delicious, and many say that it has the taste and appearance of veal. The roe is considered a delicacy. The favored method of fishing for these monsters was to use a strong cotton handline with a single hook baited with a whole blue crab. A sixteen-ounce lead sinker carried the rigging to the bottom. If you brought home a single fish, it was considered a success; however, for the average fisherman there were more unsuccessful trips than successful. Drum fishing was one of Sam's favorite pastimes, and he certainly caught his share.

The season lasted only thirty days (generally in April), and he made the most of it. I accompanied him on many of these excursions which began at about four o'clock in the morning and could last all day long depending upon how many tides you intended to fish and the weather. When Sam arose on the morning of a planned drum fishing trip the first order of business was to take a flashlight and check the Spanish Moss on a nearby live oak tree. If the moss was hanging straight down, we would go fishing. If there was even the slightest movement of the moss from the wind, everyone went back to bed. Sam knew from experience that any movement of the moss at home signaled that the water would be too rough out in the areas where we fished.

Luck

Next to going out with one or more of his three sons, my father enjoyed drum fishing with a black friend by the name of Joe "Sonny" Goodwine. Sonny lived on Polawanna Island and held the record in his day for catching the most drum fish in a single season—twenty-nine. One day my father and Sonny were fishing the "Lands End drop," which was located about where Port Royal Sound ended and the Beaufort River begins.

This "drop" is fairly small, and on this particular day there were about twenty boats anchored, tightly packed. Each boat was a wooden *bateau* and contained two or three fisherman. My father's *bateau* was the only boat there powered by an outboard motor; all of the others arrived by the use of oars. In this entire assemblage of fishermen, Sam was the only white man present. The best time to fish for drum was when the tide slacked for either high or low water. This was a high water excursion; the fishermen all arrived and dropped their anchor about an hour before the change of the tide. There was not a whisper of wind present, and the boats were close enough together that you could listen in on conversations in the other boats. High tide came and went. In all the boats present not a single drum fish bit. Just before the force of the ebbing tide reached the point where you could no longer keep your rig on the bottom, Sam hooked a large drum fish. During the fifteen or so minutes that it took to "play" the fish and bring it to gaff, there were many suggestions and words of advice from the other fishermen on how to properly bring the fish to the boat. Finally, the big fish became exhausted and came to the surface, where Sonny Goodwine gaffed it and with his massive arms swung it on board. Several minutes later, when all of the excitement of the catch had died out, one of the fishermen made a comment which was heard by all: "De wite buckra hab all de luck."

The Great Division

One Saturday in April 1940 found Sam and me with our *bateau* tied to a navigation buoy in Port Royal Sound near the western entrance to Station Creek. I was thirteen years old. It was ebb tide against a twenty-knot south wind and Port Royal Sound was kicking it up with the waves running four to five feet. In spite of these conditions, we were comfortable in Sam's twenty-foot cypress *bateau*. Constructed of cypress, it was light as a feather and took the water extremely well. The boat had been built around 1925 for Dr. A. W. Elting, a Yankee quail hunter who spent the winter months at his Pine Island retreat, which was located on the extreme eastern end of St. Helena. Dr. Elting had tired of the boat, and he sold it to Sam for fifty dollars. The boat was powered by a 1936 ten-horsepower alternate firing twin-cylinder Johnson Sea Horse outboard. Johnson called it ten-horsepower, but by the way it shoved that big *bateau,* I believe it was closer to twenty. There was not another *bateau* in Beaufort County of its equal. While tied to the buoy hoping that the wind would abate so that we could go to our intended drop at Bay Point, a boat of about fourteen feet in length slipped out of Station Creek and made its way out to us. In this boat was a friend of ours from Beaufort, and he was accompanied by two marines who were stationed at Parris Island. They were also headed for the Bay Point Rock to fish for drum. Their boat was much too small for the conditions we knew would be present at Bay Point about a mile south of us. The wind slacked a bit and with the tide starting to slow, conditions for proceeding to Bay Point improved. Now, Sam was not a man to take unnecessary chances, but a decision had to be made since it was approaching low tide—the prime fishing time. The size of his boat influenced his decision and we prepared to head out. Feeling sorry for the three men in the smaller boat, which obviously was not going to Bay Point on this day, he invited them to bring their tackle and ride with us and leave their boat tied to the buoy. This offer was accepted and away we went. In twenty minutes we anchored at Sam's favorite spot at Bay Point.

Immediately after arriving, the fish really started to bite, but not for Sam and me. Our friend from Beaufort caught a drum that was about a forty-five pounder, and one of the two marines caught two fish each with an estimated weight in excess of sixty pounds. Sam and I caught nothing. Shortly after landing those three fish we headed in, with Sam and I having the same thought—that when we reached their boat surely they would share their catch with us. After all, were it not for Sam's generosity, they would have none. Shortly thereafter we pulled alongside their boat. Sam and I were stunned when they pitched all three fish into their boat, thanked us for the trip, and told us goodbye. This was the topic of much conversation in the McGowan household for several weeks. So much for being a nice guy.

Catastrophe at Bay Point Rock

Saturday, April 26, 1947, started out as a typical Lowcountry spring day on St. Helena Island. Not a breath of air stirred to cause even the slightest ripple in Port Royal Sound or in the wide expanses of the mighty Broad River. Broad River is the largest of the tributaries which empty into Port Royal Sound; the other main tributaries are the Beaufort and Chechessee Rivers.

At dawn on this fateful day, Neff Swetman launched his fourteen-foot wooden *bateau* from the beach at Lands End on St. Helena Island for a day of drum fishing. Several hundred yards up the beach, at about eleven o'clock on this same Saturday in April, Clayton Boardman also departed for a fishing trip in his boat. Later that day, at about 2:30 in the afternoon, these two men, purely by providence, would have a momentary face-to-face encounter. Within moments of this chance meeting, one would be dead and the life of the other would be changed forever.

Normally, Neff kept his *bateau* in a small creek that comes in behind the southern tip of Lands End. This creek has been called "The Swash" since slavery times. During the month of April each year, however, Neff would move his boat to the beach at Lands End because it shortened the distance considerably to his house. Neff had no car or other conveyance and lived approximately one-half mile from this impromptu landing. April is the month in the year when the big drumfish move up the Broad River to spawn, and Neff Swetman was a superior drumfisherman. He was a powerful man, light skinned, six-feet four-inches tall, and weighed in at 235 pounds. Sam said that Neff Swetman was the strongest man, white or black, that he had ever known. Many in the Lands End area will attest that on numerous occasions, upon returning from drumfishing, Neff would put his ten-horsepower Johnson outboard motor on one shoulder and a sixty- to seventy-pound drumfish on the other and walk the half mile distance to his house without stopping.

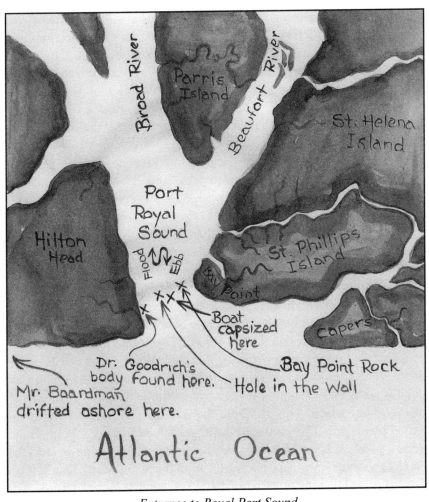

Entrance to Royal Port Sound

Ezekial Mack said that the reason Neff possessed such strength was that he was double jointed. Neff's mother was black and—according to Ezekial Mack—the source of any and all worthwhile information on the Western end of St. Helena Island. His father was a white Marine officer stationed on Parris Island. Neff's mother worked for this officer and his family and lived in his quarters during the week returning to Lands End on the weekends. Ezekial Mack also named three other men and one woman from the Lands End community, all of whom I knew quite well, who arrived upon this earth under identical circumstances. The mothers of these five people were without question exploited by their employers. Many of the black residents of the Lands End community worked at Parris Island and rowed across the Beaufort River to work rather than make the arduous sixty-mile roundtrip by land. This was not unlike a water taxi. The owner of the *bateau* charged five cents per day to ride, and the passengers performed all of the rowing. In spite of all of Neff Swetman's many physical attributes, there was one, however, in which he was totally lacking—especially for a man who spent so many hours on the water. According to Ezekial Mack, Neff Swetman could not swim, and it was this missing skill that probably cost him his life.

When Neff Swetman left the security of the Lands End beach early in the morning of the 26th of April in 1947, he was accompanied by two of his neighbors—Token and Luther Green. Token and Luther were first cousins. The men were headed for Bay Point Rock, a favorite drumfishing spot about one mile's distance from Lands End Beach. Bay Point Rock is located approximately one-half mile from the Western end of Bay Point Island. This is where the Atlantic Ocean and Port Royal Sound join hands. The width of Port Royal Sound from Bay Point to the nearest point on Hilton Head Island is approximately two miles, and the depth across this imaginary line varies from thirty to seventy feet. It is an extremely treacherous body of water if the wind velocity is above ten knots and is blowing against the flow of the current. The current flow velocity at Bay Point averages approximately seven knots.

The men arrived at Neff's favorite drop shortly before an 8 A.M. low tide and immediately took three large drum, each weighing in excess of fifty pounds. This was a signal to Neff that there was a school of drumfish present, so the decision was made to remain on the drop to fish the next slack water which would not occur until 2 P.M. The flow of the current at Bay Point Rock is so swift that the bait cannot be successfully placed on the bottom until the tide slackens for low or high water. Drumfish are strictly bottom feeders.

So they waited, occasionally catching a catnap during this four- to five-hour lull in the fishing action. The time passes very slowly when waiting for the tide to rise and fall, giving little credence to the old adage that "time and tide wait for no man." A southwesterly breeze of approximately six knots put a light chop on the surface, but this gave the fishermen little concern. There was no evidence to forewarn that a fast-moving cold front was approaching from the northwest.

The tide began to slacken at about 2 P.M. for high water, and two more large drum were taken on the handline, bringing on board an additional 120 pounds to the heavily burdened *bateau*. Shortly after bringing on board the second of the two fish taken at high tide, Neff Swetman heard the roll of thunder and saw the leading or squall edge of the cold front approaching from the northwest—straight down the open expanses of the Broad River. Instantly Neff had his man in the bow of the boat pull in their anchor while the outboard motor was being started. The boat was immediately headed toward the protective shoreline of Bay Point when one of Neff's companions called his attention to a boat anchored about one-fourth mile further out in Port Royal Sound toward Hilton Head. One of the men in the distant craft was frantically waving an object trying to attract their attention. Neff turned his boat about immediately and proceeded toward the signaling boat. Neff came alongside the craft and discovered that the two white men in the boat had a disabled outboard motor and were seeking assistance. They had also seen the approaching storm and were trying desperately to reach the safety of calm water. The disabled craft was anchored at a famous fishing spot at the entrance to Port Royal Sound historically known as "The Hole In The Wall." This spot or "drop" is a very small outcrop of phosphate rock protruding from the bottom. Small fish congregate around this outcrop and their presence attracts larger fish.

The two men in the disabled craft were Clayton Boardman, president of Boardman Oil Company in Augusta, Georgia, and a prominent physician, Doctor William H. Goodrich, also of Augusta. Mr. Boardman owned a cottage on the beach at Lands End on St. Helena Island. He was fifty-six years old. Doctor Goodrich was seventy-three years old and was a weekend guest of Mr. Boardman. Seeing that Neff Swetman's boat was already overloaded, Mr. Boardman suggested that Neff's outboard motor be placed on his craft as it was much larger. But Neff Swetman was a strongheaded man and knowing that time was of the essence with a storm fast approaching, he refused Mr. Boardman's offer. Instead, he told the two men that he was headed for the Bay Point shore, and that if they wanted a ride to get in his boat. This was the last decision Neff Swetman would make in his lifetime. Very reluctantly, Mr. Boardman and Dr. Goodrich left their anchored boat to fend for itself and clambered into Neff Swetman's boat, each man taking with him a kapok boat seat which also serves as a water flotation device. This action would also be the last decision Dr. Goodrich would ever make.

Neff Swetman cranked his motor and headed his heavily loaded *bateau* toward Bay Point, a distance of approximately three-quarters of a mile. Within two to three minutes after departing Mr. Boardman's boat, the squall struck and Neff Swetman's boat was immediately capsized. Relieved of its burden of men, fish, and other paraphernalia, the boat floated upside down, and only Luther Green managed to cling to it. Neff Swetman and Token Green, neither of whom knew how to swim, drowned immediately. Their bodies were never recovered. They presumably drifted out to sea with the tide which by the time of the accident had changed and was ebbing. Luther Green managed to cling to the overturned *bateau* for two hours tearing off all of his fingernails in the process. He was spotted by an incoming shrimp trawler and was rescued and taken to Beaufort. The *bateau* was also recovered by the crew on the trawler and towed to Beaufort. Dr. Goodrich lost his kapok flotation device in the turbulent seas and managed to stay afloat for only a few minutes before he succumbed. Mr. Boardman procured a floating metal gasoline can, but before he could throw it to Dr. Goodrich, his friend had disappeared beneath the waves.[1] Dr. Goodrich's body was discovered on the beach on Hilton Head Island at 11:30 A.M. the following morning, two miles from where the accident took place.

Clayton Boardman would endure an ordeal of unimaginable proportions for the next nine-and-a-half hours. He had managed to hang on to his kapok flotation device when the *bateau* capsized, and it would save his life. The tide had begun to ebb and was flowing seaward when the accident occurred, and Clayton Boardman was drifting rapidly out into the Atlantic Ocean. After being in the water for approximately one hour, the same trawler that had picked up Luther Green passed within 125 feet of Mr. Boardman, but in the turbulent prevailing seas it did not spot him.[2] He drifted with the current an estimated six miles into the Atlantic before the tide changed and he began to drift toward land. In his miraculous journey seaward, he passed close enough to a moored navigation buoy to grasp it, but he noticed that it was totally encrusted with razor sharp barnacles from just above the waterline downward. He correctly surmised that he would lacerate himself in many places if he

[1] "Clayton Boardman Found Alive," *Augusta Chronicle*, 28 April 1947, p.1.
[2] Ibid., 1.

tried to cling to it, possibly attracting sharks with his blood. He passed up this opportunity and his uncontrolled odyssey continued. At midnight his feet touched bottom, and he walked ashore on the beach of Hilton Head Island. He was ten miles from the scene of the accident. When Beaufort County's youthful coroner Roger Pinckney was told of the accident, he correctly predicted that one or more of the accident's victims might possibly make it to Hilton Head.[3] In 1947 Hilton Head was sparsely inhabited. So sparse was the population that the Marines from nearby Parris Island were given permission to use certain beach areas for training purposes. Mr. Boardman made his way up behind some dunes and quickly fell asleep from sheer exhaustion. Shortly after daylight on Sunday morning (April 27), several Marines discovered Mr. Boardman lying in the sand. He was quickly taken to the Marine's temporary quarters where he was provided with food and dry clothing. Word was quickly passed that Mr. Boardman was alive, and he was transported back to his cottage at Lands End on St. Helena Island.

What began as a wonderful day of fishing for five men turned into unbelievable tragedy. It is ironic that Mr. Boardman's boat, left anchored in the widest expanse of Port Royal Sound, rode out the storm without incident and was recovered undamaged.

Gigging

Gigging or "striking" flounder and other fish species at night was and still is a favorite sport for many fishermen. It was a very easy and productive way to put a meal on the table. At present, the number and size of fish taken are governed by regulation, this being made necessary by the tremendous population increases along the coast. In Sam's era there was no limit to the number of fish that could be taken regardless of the method used. All one needed for gigging was a flat-bottomed boat, preferably a *bateau*, a small outboard motor, a good light, and a gig. A gig is a fish spear usually of five prongs mounted on a sturdy lightweight pole. A good knowledge of where you are at all times is very important as this endeavor is done at night, the darker the night the better. Gigging was also an easy way for three young boys to pick up a few extra dollars. On many Friday nights my two brothers and I would leave the house at "fus dak" (first dark), returning home at two o'clock on Saturday morning with seventy-five to a hundred flounder. Sam would run us into Beaufort at about 7:30, turn us loose with our fish at the foot of Carteret Street, and return to the post office at Frogmore for the morning mail run. We were

[3] "Two Prominent Augustans Believed to Have Drowned," *Augusta Chronicle*, 27 April 1947, p.1.

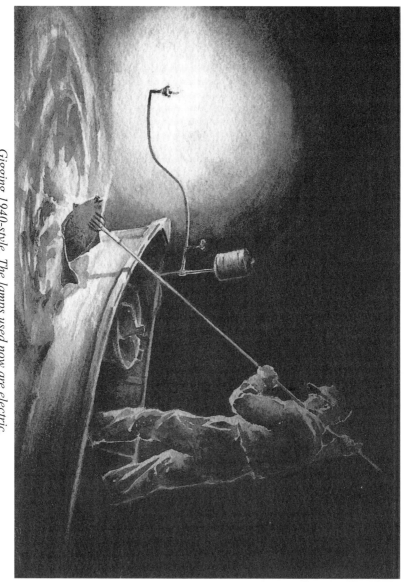

Gigging 1940-style. The lamps used now are electric.

very selective about where we peddled our fish. We sold them door to door only in "The Point." The word traveled fast, and as we turned a corner, we could look up the street and see residents waiting at the sidewalk usually with a metal dishpan in hand. A five-pound flounder or two of equal weight would bring fifty cents. In about two hours our night's catch would be gone. Our pockets would be full of cash, and I am sure there would be many smiling faces on "The Point" over a noon meal of grits and fresh flounder.

There are those who probably think that gigging is a cruel and unsportsmanlike method of taking fish. Not so. Ninety-nine percent of the time, the fish is struck in the head inflicting death almost instantly. Picture on the other hand, a five-pound redfish, or spot-tail as it's called locally, on the line. He has been placed in this position through the use of some type of artificial or other lure, and now the next three or four minutes are the most horrifying of his life. In his struggle for freedom, his remaining strength wanes, and he is brought on board only to be unceremoniously dumped into the bottom of the boat or thrown into an ice chest. Then for the next fifteen minutes or so he drowns from the lack of oxygen. Think about it.

Daylight Gigging

One night in the late 1920s Sam left our dock heading on a gigging trip accompanied by an Englishman who was in this country visiting relatives. Sam was headed for the entrance of Trenchards Inlet where it empties into the Atlantic, a distance of about five miles. About halfway there the three-horsepower motor which powered his *bateau* ran out of gas; the fuel tank on top needed to be refilled. When this occurred, Sam generally waited about five minutes for the engine to cool down before refilling. It was during this quiet respite that the Englishman, who was already very nervous about what he had gotten himself into, decided to ask Sam a question, "I say, old chap, are we there yet?"

Using this opportunity to poke a little fun at his apprehensive companion, Sam said, "Oh no. We have about eight miles to go." The Englishman responded, "My heavens, Sam. Couldn't we just head on home and finish this gigging matter tomorrow during the daylight hours?"

The City of Savannah

In August of 1893, the most disastrous hurricane of the nineteenth century struck the east coast of the United States. It came ashore midway between Charleston, South Carolina, and Savannah, Georgia, and was a very slow moving storm. Beaufort and all the local Sea Islands were squarely in the path of the storm. It was so slow in its forward movement that before one high tide had a chance to recede due to the force of the wind and wind direction, another high tide followed. The tide came so high that it is likely that less than ten percent of St. Helena Island was untouched by salt water. Inhabitants of St. Helena, Warsaw, Datha, and Coosaw Islands were drowned by the score with some estimates of the loss of life as high as one thousand. The devastation was so complete that many bodies were never found, complicating an accurate body count. The highest tides occurred at night, and it was thought by many that as the elevation of the tide began entering the occupant's homes, the occupants vacated their houses and took their chances with the elements. It was also thought that the loss of life would not have been nearly so great had the occupants remained inside their houses as the water began to rise. The majority of the deaths occurred within the black community. This unfortunate segment of the population of the Sea Islands of Beaufort County were either ex-slaves or first generation ex-slaves who lived in the poorest of housing. The hurricane of 1893 brought an end to the thriving phosphate mining industry in Beaufort County and also completed the demise of rice planting in the Lowcountry. The phosphate

The steamship City of Savannah *following her foundering during the hurricane of August 1893.*

mining industry was already on its way out due to cheaper phosphate in Florida.

Plodding along the coast of South Carolina approximately twelve miles offshore was the wooden steamship *City of Savannah*. The crew and passengers on board were totally unaware of the disaster that was about to strike. Communications and warning systems for storms one hundred years ago were almost non-existent compared with today's global satellite systems. The storm struck the *City of Savannah* with its full fury. The waves were so violent that all steerage was lost, and the little ship was driven onto a deep-water sandbar three miles off the southern tip of Hunting Island. The crew and passengers, who numbered approximately one hundred, boarded lifeboats and made it ashore on Hunting Island without loss of life. As evidenced by the photograph of the *City of Savannah*, the ship did not break apart during the storm. During the following weeks, however, from the pounding the ship had taken from the storm, its grounding, and the continual ground swells lifting and dropping the hull on the bottom, the ship broke apart leaving only its steam pistons and rudder resting on the bottom.

There is an old adage that "every cloud has a silver lining." This adage could not possibly have been truer than in the wreck of the *City of Savannah*. Over the past one hundred and five years, this wreck has been one of the premier saltwater fishing drops along the South Carolina coast, with literally millions of fish taken there. The wrecks of the ships *Lawrence* and *General Gordon* off Bay Point, as well as the *Hector* off

Fishermen standing on top of the cylinder head of the steam engine of SS City of Savannah, *January 1950.*

Georgetown, South Carolina, have also produced tons for fish to sport and commercial fisherman.

A Fishing Trip to the Savannah

In August 1940, I accompanied several friends on a three-day fishing and camping trip to the north end of Fripp Island. We established our camp on the beach of Fripp Island at a point most convenient to the wreck of the *Savannah*. Present were Julian Levin, Sam McGowan, Jr., J. C. Bishop, Dickie Fripp, my friend "Sturgeon" Mack, and me. Our boats consisted of J. C. Bishop's twenty-foot *bateau* powered by a ten-horsepower Johnson outboard and my twelve-foot *bateau* powered by a three-horsepower Bendix outboard. We slept on cots, each with its own mosquito netting supported by sticks. My companion "Studge" slept on a blanket on the ground alongside my cot also covered by my mosquito netting. Studge and I were the youngest in the group at thirteen years old.

Sam knew where we would be camping, and knowing its proximity to the wreck of the *Savannah*, gave Sam Jr. and me a very severe warning about not going to the *Savannah* without him under any circumstance. He had been out there many times and was well aware of the danger involved. So much for Sam's warning. After a great night's sleep on the beach, we awoke the next morning to a beautiful sunrise and cooked breakfast. Not a breath of air stirred. Shortly after breakfast the large *bateau* headed for the *Savannah*—a distance of about three miles out into the Atlantic. In the boat were J. C. Bishop, Sam, Jr., and Dickie Fripp. Julian Levin, Studge, and I kept our feet on solid ground. When the boat returned five hours later, three hundred pounds of fish, mostly sheepshead, were also in the *bateau*. We did not have enough ice with us to keep this quantity of fish from spoiling, so, being the youngest, I was delegated to carry the fish home for Sam, Sr. to dispose of. It was nearly sundown when Studge and I arrived home. Sam took one look at those fish and knew immediately where they were caught, but waited to hear me state from whence they came. I told him that they were caught at the old timber dock in Old House Creek behind Fripp Island where the Fripp Island Marina is now located. Now, Sam knew you could pick up a few sheepsheads at this location, but three hundred pounds in one day—no way. The truth came out.

On our way back to join our fishing companions at the north end of Fripp Island at ten o'clock that night, it was apparent that a major thunderstorm was approaching from the north. Just before it struck, I beached our *bateau* on a small hummock, and my friend and I took refuge from the storm by removing the motor and contents from the boat and dragging it up on the beach and turning it upside down. While the storm raged outside we were very comfortable underneath the boat. The storm lasted about an hour, and by midnight we had rejoined our friends.

The next morning when the larger *bateau* headed back out to the wreck of the *Savannah*, there were two new passengers on board—Julian Levin and Pierre McGowan. The sight of all those fish taken the day before had gotten to us. Studge could not swim and wisely stayed at our camp. We caught a large number of fish, and other than Julian Levin losing his breakfast overboard, the morning was fairly uneventful. Then, near disaster struck. Guarding the entrance to Fripp Inlet was a long, narrow sandbar which runs parallel to the beach. The depth of the water on top of this "bar" is about two feet at low tide with ground swells constantly breaking over it which clearly marks its location. Rather than go one-fourth a mile to the west and into the narrow opening with no breaking waves, our boat captain chose to approach the bar head on and ride over it with the waves. When we were directly over the bar, for reasons unknown, our captain released his hold on the handle of the

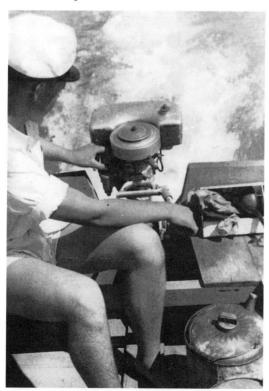

Heading home from a fishing trip to the City of Savannah, *July 1940.*

outboard. The motor swung to the left due to its propeller torque sending the bow of the boat to the right, and placing it parallel to the waves. In an instant a large swell rose up and broke over the side of the boat, completely soaking us and filling the *bateau* half full of water. The boat was already heavily laden with five fishermen and many fish, in addition to the motor and other equipment. One more such wave would have completed the job of swamping the boat. Instead, before another wave could hit us broadside, and before there was any panic, someone yelled, "Everybody overboard!" Everyone obeyed, each thinking the same thing: *How deep is the water?* We were all astounded to discover that the water was only three feet in depth. We quickly maneuvered the boat around with its bow facing the oncoming waves and pulled it backward into the quiet water behind the bar. We then bailed out the boat, climbed back in, and proceeded to our camp. Studge was sound asleep when we arrived, and even though it was only about one-fourth a mile from where we had our accident, he was totally oblivious to its happening.

After all of Sam's warnings about staying away from the *Savannah*, several years passed before Sam, Jr. and I informed him about the Fripp "bar" incident.

chapter 7
duck hunting

The Judge

Duck hunting was another of Sam's favorite pastimes. There were so many birds available in the 1920s, 1930s, and 1940s that the number you could take was unlimited. I believe that is the reason duck hunting is in the shape it is in now. It is practically a waste of time to go locally any more. Loss of habitat over the years also contributed to its demise. From the time Sam set foot on St. Helena in 1924, his favorite duck-hunting companion during the 1920s and 1930s was Judge William J. Thomas of Beaufort. The Judge had a fine camp constructed on the south end of Hunting Island. The location was at about the point where the easternmost end of the Fripp Island Bridge is located. There was a pond about two-miles north of Judge Thomas's camp that was probably one of the most prolific duck hunting spots on the east coast. More specifically, the pond was located where the "lagoon" is at present. In the 1950s, the state Wildlife Department in its wisdom decided to use this area to pump sand to the beach for "renourishment." What a waste—renourishment, that is. You are not going to stop Mother Nature from doing her thing, as witnessed by events in the winter and spring of 1998.

It was not unusual for Sam and the Judge to return to my father's house after a two-day hunt with forty to fifty Blacks and Mallards. There were so many birds they only took these two larger species, leaving the smaller birds alone. Always along on these trips was Judge Thomas's man Josephus, who was camp cook and helped carry the ducks. Judge Thomas was very fond of grits, and Josephus was required to cook them for forty-five minutes. I was privileged to make a few of these trips in the late 1930s, but only to "mind the camp." The Hunting Island trips all came crashing to an end in 1939 when the owner, Dr. A. W. Elting, donated the island to the state with the stipulation that it be used as a state park.

Duck Dinner From The Front Door

In 1938, my father procured four wild Mallard eggs from a friend of his who resided in Canada. He hatched them under one of his obliging Rhode Island Reds, and by 1941 he had approximately a hundred

Mallards of his own. These tame Mallards unwittingly became live decoys. The birds spent a lot of their time on the salt marsh out in front of our house when the tide was in, and many wild ducks would be attracted by their presence. On numerous occasions wild Mallards or Blacks would follow Sam's tame birds right into the yard. They were a little skeptical and always separated themselves a little distance from the birds belonging to Sam. Sam kept a loaded twelve-gauge double-barreled shotgun adjacent to the front door, and when the wild ducks came into range he would crack the door open and blast away. Many delicious wild duck dinners were obtained in this fashion.

One, Two, Three—Bang

When my brothers and I came of duck-hunting age, our favorite hunt was on St. Phillips Island, now owned by media magnate Ted Turner. There are dozens of ponds on this barrier island, all very narrow and running east–west. The vegetation on the pond edges is so thick that duck blinds were not required. When the wind was of any appreciable strength, it created such a noise in the numerous Palmetto trees you could sneak up on the birds and ambush them. This was our preferred method of attack.

My older brother Sam generally was privileged to use our father's twelve-gauge double while I was relegated to a single-shot twelve. We would slip up on a large flock of Mallards or Blacks who would be feeding and then execute our attack. Many of the birds would have their heads under water feeding. When everything was ready, one of us would whistle, causing all of the birds to raise their heads. At the count of three, both our guns would go off simultaneously. When the birds took flight, my brother Sam would drop another bird with his second barrel and while he was doing this, I would eject my dead shell and insert the fresh shell I had been holding in my left hand. Sometimes I would also take a bird in flight by this quick reload method. Having fired four rounds, there were numerous times we would slog back to the boat with as many as fifteen large birds. Sam would be waiting at the boat for us when we came out of the woods and would always have a humorous comment like, "Is that all you boys got? It sounded like a war going on in there."

Sam McGowan: Federal Game Warden

One day in March during the late 1930s, my father and a friend were off on a fishing trip to Trenchards Inlet (locally called "Trunkards"). The duck hunting season had been over for several months. When they arrived at the inlet they could not help but notice William Scheper's yacht the *Owanee* anchored down near St. Phillips Island. Mr. Scheper was the

Dr. Parker Jones with a brace of
Blacks on Old Island, 1956.

owner and President of The Peoples Bank in Beaufort. When they approached the boat, Mr. Scheper came out on deck, and recognizing Sam, he invited him and his friend on board. While they were on deck, they heard several shotgun blasts on nearby St. Phillips. My father asked Mr. Scheper who was doing the shooting. "Willie," as he preferred to be called, told my father that the shooting probably came from a guest of his, a new schoolteacher at Beaufort High School by the name of Parker Jones. Now when a situation like this presented itself, my father was at his best, especially if he had had a nip or two. He suggested that he and Mr. Scheper go ashore in Sam's *bateau* and try to locate Parker Jones. If they were successful in finding him, and Sam had no doubts about this as he knew St. Phillips like the back of his hand, Mr. Scheper was to introduce my father as Sam McGowan, Federal Game Warden, instead of Sam McGowan, RFD Mail Carrier. Mr. Scheper thought this was a great scheme, so away they went. They parked the *bateau* at a convenient location and went about looking for Parker Jones. In a few minutes they saw him coming down a path about fifty yards away. When Parker saw Mr. Scheper accompanied by a total stranger, he became panic-stricken.

He threw the two ducks he was carrying in one direction and the double-barreled shotgun he was carrying, which really belonged to Mr. Scheper, in the opposite direction. He then proceeded to where Sam and Mr. Scheper were waiting. As planned, my father was introduced as a Federal Game Warden. Sam had seen everything and being the woodsman that he was, he immediately retrieved the gun and ducks. On the way back to Mr. Scheper's boat, they all were very quiet and you could tell that Parker Jones was very concerned. Just out of college on his first teaching job, he could envision the Beaufort County School Board meeting to decide his fate the following week. When they were safely back on board the yacht, things started heating up. Parker had brought on board a quart of Jack Daniels and for two hours he followed Sam around keeping his glass filled. Mr. Scheper started feeling so sorry for poor Parker that he finally let him in on the secret. Parker was so relieved that he totally forgave my father. In fact, this incident created a friendship that lasted many years and evolved into many duck-hunting forays.

chapter 8
quail hunting

Sam (r) and Charleston attorney Augustine T. Smythe relax during a quail hunt, 1906.

Dr. Elting

St. Helena Island throughout the nineteenth century and until about 1970 had to be considered one of the premier quail-hunting spots in the United States. This did not go unnoticed by a young surgeon by the name of Arthur W. Elting from New York, who "discovered" St. Helena around 1900. He was an avid quail hunter and quickly realized that he had struck gold. At the extreme eastern end of the peninsula where St. Helenaville stood before the Civil War lies Pine Island. He immediately purchased it. I believe what impressed him about Pine Island which contains seventy-seven acres was its remoteness and its extremely high elevation above mean sea level. It lies approximately one-half mile out in the marsh from St. Helena, connected by a causeway which was at the time very suspect.

Pine Island is bordered on its southern exposure by Village Creek and on the east by St. Helena Sound. He quickly made improvements to the causeway and built a comfortable hunting lodge on Pine Island to accommodate his family and several guests. A black couple, Charlie and Harriet Watson, who lived in the nearby Tom Fripp community, worked for Dr. Elting most of their adult lives. Dr. Elting built a cottage for their personal use while he was here each winter. This cottage was located on St. Helena Island near the westernmost end of the causeway to Pine Island.

He then set his sights on quail hunting. By the time he was through acquiring land suitable to his quail-hunting purposes, he had locked up approximately one half of the total acreage on St. Helena. If you drew a line running north and south starting at Orange Grove Plantation and extended it to the western edge of Edgar Fripp Plantation on Seaside Road, the majority of the land east of this line was his territory for hunting. On most of this land, he leased the hunting rights from the local black landowners for ten cents an acre. When any parcel of land in the area described was sold at the courthouse door for non-payment of taxes, it was bought in his name by his local attorney Brantley W. Harvey, Sr. In 1926, he commissioned Arthur Christensen, the only local surveyor (and a Harvard and MIT graduate) to prepare a map showing all of the property owners in the eastern half of St. Helena Island. I have a copy of this map, and it is incredible to examine it and marvel at all the property he had acquired in twenty-six years. He bought entire plantations: Seaside, 944 acres; Feliciana, 448 acres; Cherry Hill, 300 acres; St. Helenaville, 90 acres; Village Farm, 200 acres; and Marion T. Chaplin, 303 acres.[1] He also purchased an estimated additional 650 acres at property tax sales. From my experiences of quail hunting on St. Helena over forty years, it is conservative to state that Dr. Elting had over 300 coveys of birds at his disposal. My father said that Dr. Elting did not shoot the same covey twice in any one hunting season. He also purchased Hunting Island, later donating it to the state (1939) for use as a State Park. And he kept on buying. By the time Dr. Elting died in 1944, he was one of the largest landowners on St. Helena, second only to Edward Gustave Sanders. It is estimated that he owned 3,000 acres and leased an additional 7,000 acres on St. Helena Island, all for the purpose of quail hunting.

I saw his hunting party only once when I was about fourteen years old. A mule-drawn wagon for hunting guests and dogs with two or three

---

[1] Theodore Rosengarten, *Tombee*, New York: William Morrow and Co., Inc., 1986, pp. 324-325.

dog handlers on horseback was the general rule. It was very impressive, not unlike the system presently used today on such places as Clarendon and Chelsea Plantations.

Sam's Turn

Upon learning of Dr. Elting's death in 1944, before you could say New York City, Sam jumped into the fray. He leased approximately 1,500 acres along Seaside Road immediately east of his residence for quail-hunting purposes, as well as some acreage in the Saxonville area of St. Helena. This acreage was considered small compared with the quail land holdings of Dr. Elting, but he leased only the best. Within this acreage Sam and I knew the location of and could find with regularity a total of about sixty coveys of native quail. Each covey at the beginning of the hunting season contained twelve to twenty birds. Sam had a very strict rule about extending the species and leaving birds for "seed." When a covey was reduced to eight birds, it was never molested again during the season. With this many available, ten to twelve coveys found on an average afternoon's hunt was the norm.

Jack hard on point, 1946.

Jack

Sam told me more than once that there is a feeling among quail hunters that during your hunting years, the Lord only permitted you to possess only one bird dog that was a real class act. Such dogs are sometimes referred to as "naturals." Sam's was named Jack. In 1945, he heard about a trainer of bird dogs living near Goldsboro, North Carolina, that had some fine, well-trained bird dogs, and he drove up there to take a look at what the man had. The trainer brought out a one-and-a-half-year-old pointer named Jack. They went out into the field where Jack immediately froze on a covey of birds. The dog's owner walked into the covey and flushed them, killing one bird with a .410 gauge shotgun. The dog did not move until ordered, at which time he found and retrieved the dead bird holding it softly in his mouth. Sam paid the man $150 for Jack and brought him to his new home at Frogmore. During the next fourteen years a bond evolved between my father and the dog, and Sam cared for him like he was one of the family.

In 1945, another big change in quail-hunting circles occurred on St. Helena. A man by the name of Archibald Randolph from Upperville, Virginia, purchased Pine Island, and with it went most of the land that had been purchased by Dr. Elting on St. Helena. He, too, was a quail hunter, and not having as much land as he wanted for hunting as the leases had been lost, he got into a suitable hunting partnership with my father. My father liked him immediately. He was from the south. Archie, as he was called, had four bird dogs of his own, all well bred, highly trained, and very expensive. The first time Archie Randolph went hunting with my father and saw Jack work, he was dumbfounded. He asked Sam to sell him the dog but the answer was no. Money was no object for Archie so he upped the ante. He was so taken with Jack he offered my father $500 for the dog. He proposed to keep him only five years, after which he would return him free of charge. Sam would also have equal hunting time with Jack during the hunting season. Sam's Scottish blood took over and they struck a deal. At the end of five years, Archie returned Jack to my father, and we hunted him another seven years. Jack died in 1958 at age fifteen. It was one of the saddest days of our lives when we laid him to rest near my father's house. The tears from both of us flowed like water. I had been in the field several hundred times with him and probably killed over a thousand quail in his company. It was as though the world had come to an end on St. Helena Island.

The Shattered Parker

Shortly after moving into the new house on Seaside, Sam acquired a bird dog that in his words was not worth killing; the dog was so sorry. Well, killing the dog was what he set out to do. Not having the stomach to perform the deed himself, he hired a local man to do the job. He handed him the dog on a leash, a shovel, his Parker double-barrel shotgun, and two shells. After receiving further instructions from my father as to where to perform this despicable act, off the man went with the dog. Soon thereafter my father heard two shots. In about fifteen minutes the man reappeared bringing the shovel, the shotgun which had the stock completely broken off, and the leash with its collar broken. The hireling explained to my father that he tied the dog to a small tree and began excavating a suitable grave. He fired the gun twice at point-blank range, missing completely both times. Afraid to return to my father's house with the job not performed he then proceeded to try to kill the dog by striking it over the head with the butt of the gun. The stock of the gun missed the dog and struck the tree to which it was tied. The dog broke the collar in its fright, escaping to its freedom leaving the man with Sam's Parker broken into two pieces. The dog was never seen again, and my mother told Sam it served him right.

Number Eight Shot in the Face

One Saturday afternoon in January of 1956, I took a friend of mine, Edward Samuel, on a quail hunt. Sam went along but not to hunt. As Ed and I hunted, he tagged along several hundred yards behind nailing up "No Hunting" signs. In his opinion you could not put up enough "No Hunting" signs in an attempt to keep the poachers out. Our dog Jack pointed a covey of birds into which we shot, each bagging a bird. We watched the covey fly for about seventy-five yards before settling into a patch of myrtles which were about waist high. It was time for "single" bird shooting.

When we flushed the initial single birds, three arose simultaneously. One bird flew to the right, which was obviously Ed Samuel's shot. The other two birds turned to my left heading directly back from where the covey first flushed. Edward fired a single shot killing his bird. I fired once at each bird killing both on my side. As I pulled the trigger on the second bird, I heard Sam yell out. Unbeknown to Ed and me, he had walked up behind us to within forty yards and a load of twenty-gauge bird shot from my first shot hit him head on. One pellet passed completely through his right ear and one pellet struck him directly between the eyes, lodging against his skull at the bridge of his nose. Approximately fifteen pellets struck him in the canvas hunting jacket he was wearing, each burning a tiny hole in the cloth. None of these pellets made it through his clothing. The ear wound bled profusely even though it was superficial. By the time I reached him, he had removed his trifocals and was rubbing his face and ear. Blood was smeared over his entire face, most of it coming from the ear wound. It appeared to me at that instant that the whole load had struck him in the face. Ed and I rushed Sam to Dr. Parker Jones's office, Parker had returned to Beaufort upon graduation from Medical School in 1950.

His office was on the first floor of his residence on North Street, and he had a fluoroscope machine in it. We looked at the location of the pellet on the bridge of his nose, and Dr. Jones made the decision to leave it where it was. The area around the pellet had become swollen, and he decided that it would be dangerous to probe for it. It gave him no trouble, and when my Sam died nearly twenty-five years later he was still carrying that pellet. Parker had made a good decision. An accident such as this is one that no matter how careful you are, you never dream that it will happen to you. In an almost identical accident on St. Helena several years later, a friend of mine at the Marine Corps Air Station, Chief Warrant Officer George Young, one of the top skeet shooters in the world, shot his hunting companion. A single pellet hit one eye and ended his flying career in the Marine Corps.

General Dead-Eye

In 1961, Sam and I added two members to our quail-hunting group, Buddie Glenn of Beaufort and his brother-in-law, Harry Lightsey, Sr., of Columbia. What an addition this was—no two finer gentlemen ever walked the face of this earth. This partnership lasted for thirteen years until 1974, when Buddie and Harry had reached the age where those long jeep rides and accompanying walks began to take their toll. Sam had already terminated his quail-hunting days when he had a heart attack in 1962. During the quail-hunting season in 1966, Buddie invited Major General Jim Masters, Commanding General at Parris Island at the time, along on a hunt. It was during this hunt that I witnessed an event that almost ended Buddie Glenn's life. We were returning to our jeep in heavy broomstraw, having just dropped several singles from a scattering of birds out of a covey. Buddie and I were walking abreast of each other with the General walking along directly behind Buddie. Unexpectedly, a single flushed from under my feet, rocketed slightly to my left and around a small clump of brush which was directly in front of us. Since it was obviously Buddie's shot, I did not raise my gun. Buddie took one step to the left in order to follow the bird's line of flight and raised his gun to fire. General Masters took two steps to his left, raised his gun, and fired. The muzzle of the gun was no further than a foot from Buddie's head. The blast to his left and rear was deafening. Buddie shot a glance at me in absolute amazement. He and I knew in an instant that had he taken two steps to the left instead of one his head would have been blown off. Not a word was spoken by anyone. About three months later at his departure party, the General spotted me and inquired as to why Buddie never invited him for a return hunt. I could feel the question coming before he opened his mouth. In order to save the General from embarrassment, I was forced to tell him that Buddie had a number of others to whom he owed a quail hunt and that he just ran out of time before the season ended. Buddie and I always wondered if the General realized what a blunder he had pulled in the field that day.

Another General

When the hunting relationship with Buddie Glenn and Harry Lightsey ended in 1974, I found another delightful man to have as my hunting partner. He came on Buddie Glenn's recommendation. Like General Masters, he was a Major General in the U.S.M.C. and was most recently the Commanding General at Parris Island, now retired in Beaufort. His name was Oscar Peatross, and we enjoyed a most entertaining hunting relationship for fifteen years. He was a recipient of the Navy Cross awarded for valor in the secret Makin Island raid in February 1942. The termination of our hunting was forced upon us by the disappearance of the quail in 1989. Peat, as he liked to be addressed, bought a very comfortable house at Ndulamo. This is the correct spelling, not what the county road sign says (Dulamo). Ndulamo was named at about the turn of the century by the headmistress of Penn School, Miss Rossa Cooley who had constructed a summer cottage there. According to local resident Lula Holmes, Ndulamo is an African word meaning "a quiet, peaceful place."

On the very first quail hunt in 1974, I warned him severely about shooting too closely around and in the proximity of the houses of those from whom we leased the quail hunting rights. In one of our numerous covey rises that afternoon, he committed the most cardinal sin of all for our style of hunting. He fired directly at a house about seventy-five yards away in the excitement of a covey rise, and I cringed when I heard the pellets hitting the tin roof. When I walked into my house that evening upon returning from hunting, Faye greeted me with the message, "You received an urgent phone call from one of your lease ladies this afternoon. She wants you to call her the minute you walk in."

I knew the lady quite well, and when I got her on the phone she said, "Pear—you bin huntin ober my way dis ebenin." I told that it was me, to which she replied, "You shoot my boy, you no."

I said, "Way I shoot um?"

She say, "You shootum in de face. I carry um in fuh see Dr. Jenkin (Dr. Arthur A. Jenkins of Beaufort) an he pull a le piece ob lead out he face. De boy is all rite, but you mus go an see Dr. Jenkin." I told her I would take care of it. What she was getting across was that I was responsible for the bill. When I called Peat he was shocked at something he had so carelessly done. From then on he shied away from the proximity of houses in our shooting territory.

Field and Stream Big Game Hunter

During the quail-hunting season in the fall of 1964, a monthly feature writer for *Field and Stream* magazine got in touch with Buddie Glenn. He was traveling through the area looking for a story, and someone in Beaufort told him we had the best quail hunting around. Buddie, being the gentleman that he was, invited him to be his guest for several days during which time we would arrange to take him quail hunting. Now this gent had with him a worn out, scruffy looking English Setter that slept on the back seat of his 1953 Oldsmobile. The back seat looked worse than the dog. Buddie had two pointers that were very close to perfection, and it fell on me to take his guest out on two long afternoon hunts. He brought his English Setter along, and that is about all you could say for the dog. The dog had long hair and most of our territory was best suited to the use of pointers which have short hair. The Setter spent most of its time sitting on its haunches pulling briars out of its hair. The two hunts were very successful, and Buddie and I waited eagerly for our story to appear in *Field and Stream* magazine. It took about a year for it to make its appearance, and Buddie and I were shocked when we read it. Most of his story had to do with how great his mutt was. The writer used such superlatives as magnificent point, eagerly trailing, smartly backing and the like. Our dogs hardly got a mention. We got the picture in a hurry that writers have to embellish their work with fictitious particulars. Sam told me that he had been on several hunts in his younger days with Archibald Rutledge and determined later in reading some of his work that he knew no bounds when it came to exaggeration. I have read only one of his writings—*An American Hunter* (1937)—and after reading it I know where Sam was coming from. Archibald Rutledge was truly the master of exaggeration and embellishment. Here are just a few of the many contained in his book—all verbatim:[2]

- *He was a ten pointer or better.*
- *The distance carefully measured was eighty-nine steps (deer killed by Rutledge with shotgun).*
- *A regal diamondback rattlesnake—eight-feet long.*

[2] Archibald Rutledge, *An American Hunter*, New York: Frederick A. Stokes Company, 1937, entire list from throughout book.

- *I have seen a string of twenty-nine rattles. (I think Mr. Rutledge is trying to impress upon the reader that this was a single rattlesnake with twenty-nine rattles. No way. If he saw a string of twenty-nine rattles they were rattles from either two or three snakes clipped together, which is not a difficult task to perform. My bet is two tens and a nine.)*
- *I killed the seven-foot diamondback.*
- *He had, I judged, eleven or twelve points.*
- *Fallen monarch of the great Pineland and the lonely swamp (turkey).*
- *A monstrous and ferocious creature (a pig).*
- *A flock of thirty Mallards swung over me. I let drive both barrels into the huddle and down came six of the splendid birds—all drakes.*
- *There lay the big buck dead from a clean shot at eighty yards (twelve-year-old boy with buckshot, the first ever shot at).*
- *Mountain Turkey–hunt-shot at two gobblers—I could see them going for a matter of two miles or more. (I do not believe that a person has been born, with one exception, that could have this kind of eyesight, especially with heavily wooded mountains in the background. According to* Jane's Encyclopedia of Aviation, *the wingspan on a Cessna 150 is thirty-two feet, eight-and-one-half inches. I doubt if you could see this size aircraft at two or more miles in mountainous country!)*
- *I saw eight gobblers—think of it, eight!*
- *A gobbler of truly lordly size.*
- *A regal gobbler.*
- *Another ten-point buck.*
- *I saw seven gobblers walk calmly across the road.*
- *Here came a ten pointer.*
- *I can recall killing not fewer than sixteen stags on last chances.*
- *Another ten pointer.*

But then again, he sold a lot of books.

The End of Quail Hunting on St. Helena

From my quail-hunting days with Sam during my youthful years, I think it is fair to estimate that in 1960 there existed a minimum of five-hundred coveys of birds on St. Helena. This is based on personal knowledge of the location of sixty coveys in our hunting territory of 1,500 acres. During the next thirty-five years a remarkable thing happened. The quail on St. Helena for the most part simply disappeared. St. Helena quail hunters with whom I have discussed this phenomenon seem to agree that the loss of and change of habitat were probably the biggest culprits. During the golden years of quail hunting on St. Helena, most of the land was taken up with small mini-farms owned and operated by the descendents of slaves freed by the Civil War. These farms varied in size from two to twenty acres and literally supported the quail crop. These little farms kept the land open and provided the most natural quail habitat imaginable. They planted primarily corn, peas, rice, okra, sweet potatoes, cotton, and tomatoes. Around every house on St. Helena were one or two coveys of quail, and as a general rule there was a thicket nearby for protection from predators.

Starting in about 1960, these small farms began to diminish in number as the occupant's livelihood was being provided by other endeavors. Thousands of acres of once productive farmland lay fallow. The annual burning, plowing, and planting of the land was gone and the land soon grew up in brush. Farmer and premier St. Helena quail hunter Jack Dempsey believes that the annual burning of farmland and adjacent woodlands is one of the key ingredients to quail production. I gave up quail hunting about ten years ago due to the lack of birds while Jack Dempsey hunted on for several more years. Jack disagreed with me completely, believing that predators such as cats and hawks were a part of the problem.

While farming was declining at a rapid pace, there was another event taking place which I believe hastened the demise of this hardy little bird and quite possibly was the most contributing factor—the fire ant. Quail populations have declined remarkably in many other areas of the state. A friend and quail hunter, Norman Shepard of Williamsburg County, lays the blame for the decimation of his birds squarely on the back of this illegal alien from across the Mexican border. The fire ant theory is based on the fact that the female bird constructs her nest on the ground primarily in broomstraw. If she makes the fatal mistake of nesting in the immediate proximity of a fire ant nest, then it is just a matter of time. No molestation occurs until the eggs begin to hatch, and at this time the ants attack instantly, killing and devouring the chicks. I have demonstrated this with a dead fresh crab and minnow, and it is incredible how fast the carcass is reduced to a skeleton.

It has been three years now since I have seen a single quail where my wife and I live and where two coveys used to reside.

chapter 9
sex on st. helena island

This topic was rarely discussed during my brothers' and my formative years, but we always managed to know when something was going on.

The Harley

When my older brother Sam left home for Clemson in the fall of 1941, he departed on a Harley-Davidson. Now, in those days, trips home from college were few and far between, and he did not show his face again until the Christmas holidays, and it turned out to be an extremely short visit.

On the date for his expected arrival, we knew it would not be until nine or ten o'clock in the evening when he arrived, so every now and then one of us would give an anxious look down our long driveway. Finally, at about 9:30, we saw the headlight of his machine approaching and in a moment he wheeled into our yard. When he dismounted, my mother was quick to notice that there was another person sitting on his motorcycle, and she was also quick to notice that it was not a man. He bounded up the stairs to the front door where my mother greeted him with a kiss and then immediately inquired as to the status of the person seated on the Harley. He told her it was a girl he picked up coming through Abbeville and that she needed a place to stay for a couple of days. She told him to get on his motorcycle and take her where he picked her up as she was not spending the night in her house. Sam got on his machine, fired it up, and roared out of the yard. We did not see him again until spring break. That is how that French mother of ours handled a situation like this.

Timely Advice

In the summer of 1940 a friend of ours who lived on St. Helena, a man in his early twenties, pulled into our yard in his 1936 Ford. He asked for my mother, and I responded that she was in the house and to go on in. An extremely worried look covered his face. In about a half an hour he came out still wearing that worried look, got into his car, and left. I went inside and asked my mother what that was all about. She said he told her that his girlfriend had all of a sudden discovered that she was in a "family way" and wanted her advice on what to do about it. She told him there was only one thing he could do: marry her. So he did.

"Tick tock, tick tock"

The Swiss Movement

Very little of any magnitude on St. Helena escaped my father's sharp eye. There was a lady who resided on St. Helena whose antics were so open that anyone with an eye for the obvious was aware of what was going on. The lady was unmarried and had a respectable number of suitors: some married, some unmarried. Now, the lady was not attractive, and there were those on the island, particularly the ladies, who wondered what the attraction was. My father, who was never at a loss for words and theories, said that he thought he knew her secret. He said he believed the lady possessed one of the principal qualities of an expensive fine-tuned watch and was possibly blessed with what he referred to as the "Swiss Movement." This is directly related to another one of Sam's truisms: that ladies who were not particularly attractive were not much in a crowd, but were hell in a corner.

Seven Months Baby

There was a couple on the island who was blessed with a baby only seven months after they got married. This was all explained away very simply by the wife who said seven month babies ran in her family. Of course.

Age—No Barrier

One day Sam was having lunch at Buddie Glenn's house along with other invitees—Rivers Varn, Beanie Trask, and Col. Bolt Webber. Now Sam was about seventy-five at the time and was the "elder statesman" of the group as the others were about fifteen years younger on average. Out of the blue, Beanie Trask posed the following to Sam: "Sam, you are a good bit older than the rest of us—tell us if you don't mind, when does everything come to a screeching halt?" In a split second, Sam, having caught the significance of the question, replied, "You'll have to ask someone older than me." And Viagra was not available in the 1960s.

Separate Rooms

Faye and I got married in July 1950 after a courtship of two years. Several months after we were married, we came to Frogmore to spend the weekend with my parents Sam and Nancy. Would you believe that French mother of mine made us sleep in separate bedrooms? So she thought.

chapter 10
illicit whiskey on st. helena

Bootleg whiskey was so-called because its manufacture was illegal, and it was also easy to transport by sliding a pint or half-pint bottle of it down one's boot without its detection. It is quite possible that the most prolific illegal whiskey producing area in the United States during the period 1920–1965 was St. Helena Island, South Carolina. During this period, this vocation possibly ranked third behind farming and fishing. Sam and I were aware of the location of five active stills in the three-square-mile-area in which we had quail-hunting rights. By applying this to the approximately thirty-square-mile-area of St. Helena, it is not considered unreasonable to assume that there were as many as fifty active stills producing illegal corn whiskey. In addition there were a few more stills located on hummocks and larger islands lying out in the marshes adjacent to St. Helena. The only access to these was by boat, and they were located so as to be beyond the reach of Sheriff Ed McTeer and his two deputies.

In 1950, the going price for a gallon of St. Helena Island produced whiskey was eight dollars. At this price the profit was enormous, considering the cost to manufacture. It required about 100 pounds of sugar and two bushels of corn to produce fifty gallons of the liquid or "mash" that would be distilled into about twenty gallons of whiskey. Sugar cost five cents per pound and corn cost seventy-five cents per bushel. Some of the "bootleggers," as they were called, raised their own corn which diluted the cost even further. Water was a major ingredient, but was generally obtained at the site of the still by digging an open shallow well. The water in many of these surface wells was contaminated, but the distilling process eliminated these impurities. There was no fuel cost incurred in the "cooking" part of the process since wood was used, which was also readily available at the site. The most highly sought wood used for firing the stills was the dead limbs from the fronds from Palmetto trees. These were found in great abundance and burned very quickly; consequently large quantities were required. For an outlay of about seven dollars and a little work, the profit would be $150 per batch.

In 1941, disaster struck the illicit whiskey manufacturing business and the legal whiskey distilleries as well. Sugar, one of the main ingredients in whiskey making, became extremely scarce and was rationed by the U.S. Government. During the war years of 1941–1945, the availability of sugar almost dried up. Ingenuity quickly provided a suitable substitute, although large quantities were required and the end product was not nearly as potent. There was not a store in the county that did not sell molasses and cane syrup, the liquid from which sugar is distilled. There were many storeowners who probably wondered why large purchases of these two items were being made. There were also many storeowners who knew exactly why such enormous quantities of molasses and syrup were being purchased and made sure that there was plenty on hand. There was a drawback, however, to the use of these two substitutes for sugar. While sugar was sold in cloth or paper bags which were easy to dispose of, molasses and cane syrup was sold in quart and gallon size cans. At the site of the stills, there were now large piles of empty cans which made it easier to detect the location of some of these illicit operations. Another sure giveaway to a still's location was the distinctive odor while the "cooking" operation was in progress. If you happened to walk within three-hundred yards downwind of a still in operation, you could follow the source of the smell to its origin with no difficulty.

A typical whiskey still on St. Helena Island was remarkable in terms of its simplicity and operation. The cost for all of the various components was virtually nothing. An operation generally included four empty fifty-five-gallon steel drums—three for aging the "mash" to fermentation of its contents and one for distillation. The three fermentation drums each had one end removed and were buried in the ground with the open end up and approximately level with the surface of the earth. Into each of these three drums was added 100 pounds of sugar and two bushels of corn for a batch. The drums were then filled with water and covered with boards or gunny sacks. The drums were buried in the ground to help keep the mash cool while it was fermenting.

The corn floated on top at the beginning of the fermentation period, but when all of the corn had made its way to the bottom, which took about seven days, the mixture was considered ready for distilling. When the mash was considered to have reached its maximum potency or fermentation stage, it was then withdrawn with a bucket and transferred to the "cooker" or distillation unit. The stills varied in capacity and configuration depending upon the size of the operation. The distillation vessel was usually a fifty-five-gallon steel drum or a portion thereof, or it was an old discarded automobile radiator. My close friend and confidant Joe "Crip" Legree said that his last cooker, approximately thirty years ago, was made out of pure copper and made good whiskey. He said he nearly cried when he saw all the axe holes punched into it when his still was finally discovered by the law. "Crip" broke his left leg when he was six years old and his parents had neither the means nor the money to get him into Beaufort to a doctor; consequently, the leg healed itself. When it finally healed, it left him with a limp, hence the name "Crip." He is now seventy-five years old and still lives in the Hopes community on St. Helena Island within fifty yards of where he was born. His daughter Bernice Wright is Beaufort County's highly successful Tax Assessor.

Joseph "Crip" Legree, master fisherman, crabber, and whiskey maker

Joe said that near the end of his whiskey-making days he had switched to the use of rye because it made better tasting whiskey. A fire was then built under the distillation vessel and stoked until the fermented liquid within was brought to a boil. The steam which was generated by this operation was then allowed to pass through a one-half or three-quarter-inch diameter steel or copper pipe, which in turn passed through a wood box (or trough) filled with water. The passage of the steam through the water-cooled pipe converted it to a liquid which was collected by gravity flow into a container. This liquid was almost pure alcohol and was the end product being sought. The higher the quality of the fermented mash, the higher the alcohol content of the corn whiskey. This clear liquid was then "cut" with water in order to make it agreeable to the taste of the consumer. All such whiskey produced on St. Helena Island was appropriately called "Scrap Iron" by manufacturers and consumers alike.

Practically all of the whiskey produced in stills on St. Helena Island and on the adjacent smaller islands was very inferior in quality, and much of it was lethal. Sam said that all whiskey produced in which an old automobile radiator was employed as the cooking vessel was a deadly potion. Many radiators manufactured during the first half of the twentieth century contained about as much lead as copper in their construction. Lead was then consequently passed along in the distillation process and thus into the bodies of the consumers. Sam believed that many St. Helena Island residents died of lead poisoning from ingesting lead through the consumption of illicit whiskey. I am not aware of any of the St. Helena Island homemade corn whiskey having been analyzed as to its alcohol content, but as inferior as it was in quality, it was a potent brew. Many Saturday night cutting and shooting scrapes had their origin in the consumption of this powerful brew. By contrast, insofar as the construction of the "cooker" or still was concerned, I do not believe you would find an illegal still in the mountains of North Carolina in which the entire apparatus was not made of pure copper.

In the three-square-mile area of St. Helena Island on which Sam and I hunted quail, many times we would find ourselves in close proximity to one or more still in operation. We would always stop by and exchange pleasantries with the still's owner and his helpers. A sample of their product would be offered and it was considered impolite not to accept. If there was a guest with us, the owner of the still would be a little suspicious, but not unduly concerned. There was an unwritten pact between hunter and still owner which simply put was: "if hunnah gwine shoot de bud on we lan, den hunnah ain no nuttin bout dis still." "Hunnah" is Gullah for the pronoun "you." One Saturday afternoon during the quail-hunting season in 1964, my hunting companion was noted attorney Harry M. Lightsey, Sr., from Columbia, South Carolina. We had flushed a covey of quail, which then scattered into the brush on the edge of the shoreline of St. Helena. We became separated in our search for these elusive creatures, and Harry's foray had taken him very close to a still that was in operation. The owner of the still, peeking out from his hideaway, saw a man approaching who was totally unfamiliar to him. He approached Harry, and in an attempt to steer him away from the still, pretended that he was searching for a lost horse, and asked Harry if he had seen the animal. Harry Lightsey hunted with us regularly and had been advised that this event might occur one day. He simply told the man that he had not seen the horse, or anything else, turned, and walked away. Sheriff Ed McTeer and his two deputies knew the location of many of the stills and would make a raid several times a year. Rarely would anyone be caught because in the black community word of such matters spread as though by magic. In addition, when the word got around that a raid was on, the still's main operating pieces would have disappeared by the time the deputies arrived. Two days later the still would be back in operation at a slightly different location.

The manufacture of illicit whiskey on St. Helena Island evolved from simple economics. I believe that there was as much whiskey brewed for home or self-consumption as was made for sale. The white man had the financial resources to purchase his whiskey from legal sources. The black man who was without the necessary resources simply made his own whiskey, even if it was illegal. There was very little risk involved, as Beaufort County was too large and too remote to be adequately covered by the Sheriff and two deputies. Illicit whiskey manufacture was low on the priority list as far as law enforcement was concerned. The consumption of alcohol has been around for centuries as the beverage of choice for putting one's mind at ease. Alcohol has probably caused the untimely deaths of more persons than all other drugs combined, and it seems it will always be available. The manufacture of illegal whiskey on St. Helena Island came to an end around 1970. The economic status of much of the black population of St. Helena Island had improved to the point where it was not necessary to take any risk manufacturing whiskey. Besides, there was now a deputy sheriff lurking around every corner. Also, I believe that the drinking populace was becoming wary of the consumption of the poor quality whiskey when better whiskey or beer could readily be purchased legally. It is doubtful that there is a single illicit still in Beaufort County today; however, if Prohibition were to return tomorrow, within thirty days there would be many stills turning out some form of home brew.

chapter 11
st. helena tales

Fixum

For a rural mail carrier there is nothing more important than your vehicle, and it must be kept in excellent repair in order to fight the daily pounding on the mail route. The day before the Fourth of July, 1942, Sam was in the Ford maintenance shop (which was located on Bay Street in Beaufort where Beaufort Office Supply is now located) having some work performed on his car. Now, in those days, the Fourth of July to the black population of St. Helena Island was a day of the ultimate in celebration. The majority of the black population would gather at Frogmore for this event. It is difficult for me to describe how important this day was. I remember once asking a black neighbor and close friend my age (fourteen) what he was going to do on the Fourth. He excitedly responded, "Man, Ise gwine to de Fot Ob July." This meant that for the first time in his life, he was going to the celebration at Frogmore—three miles away. A band was imported from Savannah. There would be greased pig and greased pole contests, as well as the consumption of lots of food and drink. The food was prepared by St. Helena inhabitants and sold from "stands," each with its own table covered with an immaculate white tablecloth. A considerable portion of the "drink" was also prepared by St. Helena inhabitants, as at this point in history on St. Helena, there were probably more illicit whiskey stills than automobiles. The primary meat dishes were fried chicken and fish sandwiches. As Sam was waiting for his car to be repaired, he overheard a black friend from St. Helena whose car was broken pleading with the shop manager to get it repaired that day so that he might have it for the Fourth. The shop manager tried to explain to the man that he could not possibly have his car ready until the following week. Not giving up, the black man begged, "Please Suh, fixum jes so de ting will roll."

Instant Crismus

One Christmas Eve my father was standing on the sidewalk on Bay Street in front of Hugh Gray's Liquor Store talking to Mr. Gray. A black man from St. Helena Island came out of the store with a pint of whiskey he had just purchased from the clerk inside. He placed the bottle under his arm while he paused to light a cigarette, and in doing so he dropped the bottle, which smashed when it hit the concrete pavement. Not a word was spoken as the three men watched the whiskey trickling toward the gutter. Finally, when the black man realized that others were aware of this tragedy, he looked up and exclaimed, "Grate Gawd, wite folks, Crismus dun cum an gone."

William F. Scheper's yacht Owanee

Tainted Bottle

On a cold weekend during January in the mid-1930s, Sam went down to Trenchards Inlet accompanied by three close friends to do a little duck hunting on Eddings Island. The men accompanying him were brothers. Upon reaching the inlet, they quickly spotted Mr. Willie Scheper's yacht, the *Owanee*, anchored adjacent to the place where they planned to pitch their tent and spend several nights. Mr. Scheper hailed them and invited them to come on board. He knew everyone in my father's party quite well, and having ample room on board his spacious boat, invited them to stay with him and his several guests. Two days later after an enjoyable stay with Mr. Scheper and his party, my father's group made preparations to leave. Now, Sam, while he was on board, had determined that one of Mr. Scheper's guests, a banker from New York City, had a case of expensive whiskey stashed under his bunk. Sam decided that it would be nice if he and his companions had a bottle to share on the way home. Accordingly, just before departure, he slipped down to the guest's stateroom and confiscated a bottle of the man's whiskey. What Sam did not know was that one of the bottles in the case contained water. The guest, if he awoke in the wee hours of the morning and needed a drink of water, knew exactly where to get it without getting out of his warm bed. Unknowingly, this was the bottle that Sam took. The weather was very cold, and Sam had no problem concealing the bottle in his heavy hunting coat. Farewells were spoken and Sam and his friends departed the *Owanee*. They were quickly out of sight of the *Owanee* when Sam surprised his friends by producing the stolen bottle. They all were delightfully surprised at Sam's ability to pull such a caper. Sam uncorked the bottle and handed it to one of his friends for the initial drink of this illicit whiskey. His friend realized it was water from the instant it touched his lips, but thinking that Sam was pulling a joke on them decided he would continue the joke. He drank from the bottle as though it were the last bottle on earth, half emptying it. Sam and the others looked on in amazement. The bottle was then passed to another who spat it overboard upon taking a sip. When all four were finally aware of the presence of the water, a good laugh was had by all, and also a lesson learned. I'll bet the banker wondered for a long time what happened to his bottle. After all, who would take a bottle of water?

Ezekial Mack, the sage of St. Helena Island

E Han Bin on De Ax

During the month of April each year, I take an eighty-four-year-old friend of mine, Ezekial "Theodore" Mack, out to the drumfish drops several times. Theodore loves to fish for these monsters with the handline, having done it all his life, but he can no longer go by himself due to his age and physical condition. We have been doing this each year now for about fifteen years. We don't catch any fish, but we like each other's company; and while nothing is going on, which is most of the time, we solve many of the world's problems. Several years ago while out on one of these excursions, a thought came across my mind concerning an event that took place on St. Helena many many years ago; and I decided to see what, if anything, Theodore might possibly know about it. I said, "Theodore, you member back in 1945 a black lady bin git kill down on yo en ob de Islant wid she own ax?"

He say, "Sho, man. Dat oman head bin sprit opon wid e on ax."

"Well, Theodore," I said. "My pa, de minit he yeddy bout dat killin, he say he blebe he no who do de ting and he call de man name." And I told Theodore who my father suspected was the murderer.

Instantly, Theodore's reaction was "Oh no, man, dat man ain be fo kill dat oman. But he han bin on de ax! Dat oman bin kill on a Satday mawnin fo day clean. De day befo, on Friday ebenin, dat man tek to of de mens wa bin wuk fo him an gib um fifty dollar an a quat ob likker eche, an tellum ifin dey ain bin fo do de job dat nite—doan com bak fo wuk on Monday. An de nex day wen dey duz fine de body, McTear (the sheriff) he cum fo check out de ting. An he no who be de rite man, but he cah prove um. Now all dead. In twenty fo hour afta dat ting happen, ebry black man wa bin lib on de Ilant, no who kill dat oman. But ebry mout stay shut."

After hearing Theodore's version, I am positive Sam's suspicions were on the mark.

The Corsair Crash

One Saturday morning in June, 1943, I was assisting Sam in his annual ritual of completely disassembling his 1936 Johnson ten-horsepower outboard. It was really a joy to watch him do this since he was such a perfectionist when it came to maintaining his hunting and fishing equipment. In order to remove the accumulated salt build-up on the walls of the cooling tubes, he had to take the engine completely apart. I was really more of an observer than assistant. At approximately 10 A.M. an explosion took place about a quarter of a mile away which shook the ground. We ran out of the boathouse which was located at the water's edge and looking east saw a giant black ball of smoke and a parachute floating down. The parachutist was almost on the ground and was in line with the southern shoreline about one-half-mile away. I was wearing no shoes and only a pair of shorts, but I took off running as fast as I could go. In what seemed like only several minutes, I had reached the point where I estimated the pilot should be but saw nothing. There was a field

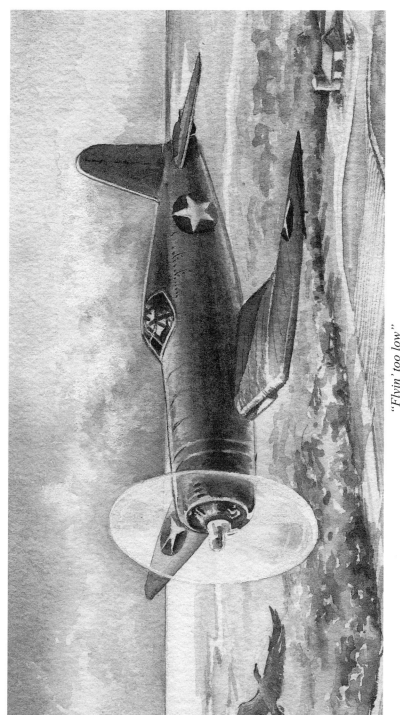

"Flyin' too low"

of corn growing practically down to the water's edge, about head high, and I saw movement in the stalks about fifty yards away. I knew I had found him.

When I approached him, a sight greeted me I shall never forget. The pilot was on all fours on the ground crawling around trying to find his flight jacket for a cigarette. His face was a mess. The first thought that entered my mind was that something had exploded inside the cockpit hitting him all over the face with tiny shrapnel-like pieces of metal. My thinking was close. He was flying a Chance-Vought F4U Corsair fighter aircraft from Page Field at nearby Parris Island. I already had that figured out from the moment of the explosion due to their daily flights overhead and besides, his wingman was overhead at about a thousand feet flying in a tight circle watching every move. The young Marine pilot (he was only two years older than me) told me they were flying west heading back toward Parris Island at five hundred feet when his aircraft collided with a large bird. He told me he saw the bird, but they were flying a little better than two hundred fifty knots, and he could not maneuver his aircraft out of the way so as to avoid a collision. The bird struck the aircraft directly on his windshield, and the little pieces of glass from the impact rendered him temporarily blind and also made numerous tiny cuts in his face. His face looked like a piece of raw hamburger. As it turned out, his most significant wound was a large gash on his left thigh that he received when he made contact with the aircraft's rudder as he bailed out. It was extremely fortunate that his leg was not broken. He was so nervous that he had removed all his clothing down to his waist. I retrieved his flight jacket and lit a cigarette for him. I then retrieved his other clothing, gathered up his parachute, and led him by the hand to a friend's house several hundred yards away. The man had an old Ford into which we piled and headed for what I thought was going to be a trip to the Navy Hospital at Parris Island. When we reached Frogmore, we met the ambulance from Parris Island into which we transferred our patient. Not a word of thanks was ever received for our efforts, but I didn't need any thanks.

My thanks would come in a few minutes. It was souvenir time, and I went dashing back to the site of the crash. The aircraft hit the ground at an angle estimated to be about thirty degrees with the horizontal. The largest single piece left of the aircraft was that monstrous eighteen-cylinder Pratt and Whitney radial engine. After the initial contact with the ground which tore a hole approximately thirty feet in diameter, the engine traveled fully five-hundred yards becoming airborne twice in its travel. The impact and accompanying explosion were so great that some of the local residents thought that "war" had surely come to Frogmore. Several reportedly fled into nearby swamps where they remained hidden for several days. The six fifty-caliber machine guns which had been wing-mounted were scattered everywhere. I knew it would be only a matter of several hours before the Marines from Parris Island would arrive to remove the debris, so I had to act fast. I hid one of the machine guns in a nearby thicket and walked home with the aircraft's gyroscope. Several days later I got one of my friends to help me in getting my other "treasures" home. The barrel of the machine gun was bent, but that didn't make any difference. About ten years later my trophies were all thrown out in one of those clean-up Saturdays.

At the age of sixteen, I never thought to obtain the name of the pilot of that aircraft. Forty-six years later, I found out his name—it was Reynolds. In 1989, there was a reunion held at the Marine Corps Air Station Beaufort for personnel of Marine Fighter Squadron VMFA 312. On a hunch I called the commanding officer of this squadron and related this story to him thinking it would be truly remarkable if this pilot made it to the reunion. He thanked me, took my name and telephone number, and said he would circulate my story at their party the following evening. The next morning when I returned from church, Faye greeted me with, "You just missed a phone call from an old Marine pilot who was at that party last night. He is headed back to his home in Maryland, but he very much wants to have a talk with you before he leaves." In a few minutes he called back and identified himself as not the pilot that I had given assistance to forty-six years earlier, but his wingman who circled overhead immediately after the accident and who was flying alongside when the bird struck the aircraft. It was during this conversation that I learned the pilot's name.

I said to him, "Tell me what became of Lt. Reynolds, and please don't tell me he was killed in the Pacific by a Japanese fighter pilot." He related to me that a tragedy happened to Lt. Reynolds that was worse than being shot down in combat. He said the Marine Corps would not let him fly for six months following the accident on St. Helena. Shortly after regaining flying status at Parris Island, he was permitted to fly a Corsair to an airport near his home in Ohio to get in some flight time. I believe this was a fairly common practice in the Army Air Corps, the Navy, and the Marine Corps. He refueled the aircraft and, in the presence of a gathering of high school friends and his family, took of to demonstrate the speed and maneuverability of the Corsair however, he crashed and was instantly killed. I thought to myself what a tragic ending to his life, particularly after that near-death collision with a bird.

Etta

In March 1977, it was time once again to mail out lease checks to the landowners on whose property we hunted the elusive quail. This chore was always done in March for the preceding hunting season, and there were sixty-five checks to be sent. These were mailed at the Frogmore Post Office with each letter bearing only the recipient's name and address, for example: Rosemary Brown, Seaside Road, Frogmore, South Carolina. For seventy years this was all the information the rural carrier needed. Well, in 1976, the post office, in its wisdom, assigned a box number to everyone having a rural address. I was not made privy to this information and mailed out those checks as usual. Every single envelope was returned within three days. With the help of a friend, Henry Williams, who knows everything, we were able to track down all the new box numbers. Out they went again, and this time only one was returned due to having a wrong box number. This one was addressed to Etta Polite. We were living in Beaufort at the time, and I decided I would deliver this one in person since I was headed to St. Helena on Saturday to work on my dock.

Our youngest daughter Kelly accompanied me. We pulled into Etta's yard on Saturday morning, and as I was preparing to knock on her door, the door opened and there she stood. Etta was seventy-five years old at the time. I gave her the check, we exchanged pleasantries for several minutes, and I turned to leave. When I reached the bottom of her steps, she called out, "Mista Pear!"

I turned and said, "Yeah Etta. Wa be de trouble?"

She said, "I wah see you bout sumpsin." I walked back up the steps thinking, the shooting rent is going up. She stunned me with, "My name ain always ben Etta yo no."

I said, "Oh, way yo name bin?"

She say, "Yo daddy gib me dis name."

I responded, "How he do dat?"

She said, "One day wen I ben a le gal bout twelbe, my ma sen me out to de rode fuh meet yo pa, fuh mail a box to Nu Yawk. I gone out deh an wate an about thuty minit later, I see um bin cumin dung de rode. He pull up longside me an I gib um de box an de muny. I stat fuh tun roun fuh go home wen yo pa hale me. He ax me wah my name bin an I tellum ma name be Henrietta Polite, Suh. Yo pa, he tek dat name an roll um roun in he mout an say, 'Henrietta, Henrietta. Grate Gawd, gal, dat name bin too long. Les short um to Etta.' I tell my ma wah yo pa say an mah name bin Etta ebber sence." Etta died in January 2000 at age ninety-eight.

The Bus Wreck

The worst traffic accident ever to happen on St. Helena Island occurred on Christmas Eve, 1950. A bus carrying civilian workers from their jobs on Parris Island overturned on the Lands End Road, directly in front of The Chapel of Ease, instantly killing eight of the thirty-eight passengers on board and seriously injuring many more.

Several years ago while drum fishing with my friend Ezekial Mack, I asked him if he recalled that accident. Ezekial replied, "How yo meen man? I bin on dat bus! Wen dat bus leabe Parris Ilant, dat bus bin fuh carry thutty seben people. Wen we cum tru Bufut on de way hom, de driber who be name Brown, he tun lef on Scott Skreet an pak in frunt ob de ice house." Ezekial continued, "De driber bin stop de bus an ebry body wa bin on de bus bin git off fuh shop fuh Crismus. Wun sumbody bin fuh buy a shree hundut pung bloc ob ice an puttem in de bac do ob de bus. Wen de bus stat fuh lod up fuh cum home, I bin de las man on, an dey ain be no seet fo me. Sumbody dun sneek on de bus wile e ben pak cause wen we leabe Parris Islant, ebry body duz hab seat. I haffa stan by de bus do an hole on to de pipe wah ben deh. We cum on cross Lady Islant an tru Frogmo. Sum ob dem boy bin fuh pick up a bottle in Bufort an bin fuh drink. We cum on tru Penn an jus fo we git to Fait Church (Faith Memorial Church opposite the Chapel of Ease), to ob dem boys bin fuh fite an wun ob dem duz fall on top de diber. He weel gon to de rite and de bus stat fuh tun ober. De bus tun on he side, and de top ob de bus duz run slap into a berry lage pine tree wa bin on de side ob de rode. Wen I see wa ben fuh happen, I hole on dat pipe. I blebe dat shree hundut pung bloc ob ice duz kil mos ob dem people wah bin ded. I ain bin fuh git nary scratch. Wun ob my shu duz git los an I ain fine um yit. Ebry time I go roun dat corner my eye duz look on de groun fo see if dat shu bin deh."

Two Flats and Out of Gas

One Sunday in 1939, I can't recall the exact date, Sam and Nancy invited three couples who were close friends over for dinner. The dinner hour was set at 7 P.M. At about ten o'clock that morning, three men who were friends of Sam's came by and spirited him off. And I mean exactly that, because spirits were definitely involved. The guests arrived at 6:30 P.M. and Sam had not returned. At seven o'clock, in spite of Sam's absence, Nancy served dinner. I knew that big trouble was brewing. In an attempt to warn Sam of the disaster which was about to fall, at about 7:30 P.M. I crept down to the basement where I could watch through a window for his arrival. At eight o'clock I saw the headlights of the car coming down our driveway, and I beat it outside to meet him. In his afternoon of fooling around with his friends, he had totally forgotten the dinner party. We went down into the basement, where I had stashed a cup of cold black coffee for him. We then sat on the basement steps for several minutes while Sam gathered his thoughts and tried to come up with a believable story when he went upstairs to face the music.

Since it was Sunday and no filling stations were open on Sundays in those days, he went upstairs, apologized for his tardiness, and then explained away the problem by stating that the car had run out of gas and on top of that they had two flat tires. I don't think there was one person in the room that night that bought his story. After the guests had departed, I was witness to one of only three times in my life where my mother berated my father, and it was a jewel. The only problem was that on the few occasions of such admonishment, she would unconsciously slip into French which Sam could not understand. He would simply nod his head approvingly as though he was agreeing with everything she said. On Thursday of the following week, one of the ladies present at the dinner party wrote Sam a most unkind and threatening letter. The letter even suggested unfaithfulness. Now, my two brothers and I would tell you straight up that Sam McGowan drank hard, played poker until two in the morning above the Ritz Café (now the John Cross Tavern in Beaufort) with his wife and children waiting in the car down below, and hunted and fished when he pleased. But be unfaithful to that beautiful French wife of his? Never.

A Foolish Mistake—At The Mercy of A Storm

Sam McGowan was not a man to trifle with when it came to the care of his hunting and fishing equipment. It was a rare occasion when he would permit any of his three sons the use of his ten-horsepower Johnson outboard. That was primarily why he bought me the three-horsepower Bendix, so I would not pester him about the Johnson ten. My friend and hunting companion of forty years, Ralph Davis, Jr., says that some of the older inhabitants of Wadmalaw Island, where he was raised, still refer to an outboard motor as an outdoors motor. Many times, Sam reiterated to his sons that there were five things that you never, ever, permitted the loan of: your wife, your outboard motor, your bird dog, your shotgun, and your cast net, and not necessarily in that order. The chain saw was later added to this list, bringing the total to six. He was a firm believer that if you lent any of the above items, when they were returned they would not be in as good condition.

So it was with great reluctance that Sam permitted me the use of his ten-horsepower Johnson outboard and twenty-foot cypress *bateau* in

August 1947, to take a fishing trip of three days' duration to the north end of Pritchards Island accompanied by friends Heyward Jenkins and Christie Cummings, both of Beaufort. During World War II the U.S. Coast Guard had constructed a wooden structure of sufficient size in which to provide comfortable living quarters for approximately ten men on each of three of the "barrier" islands off Beaufort. These were constructed on the south-end of Fripp Island, across Skull Inlet on the north end of Pritchards Island, and on the south-end of Bay Point Island. A fourth contingent of coastguardsmen were housed in abandoned Civilian Conservation Corps dormitories on Hunting Island. The men stationed in these remote locations were there for the purpose of watching the coast for possible intruders or spies put ashore from German submarines. The men on Hunting Island were provided with horses for beach patrol work, while the men on the other islands were provided with German Shepherds and Doberman Pinschers for their beach patrolling. Locally they were referred to as the horse patrol or the dog patrol. Ed McTeer, the sheriff of Beaufort County, was given a temporary commission as commander in the Coast Guard and was placed in charge of the island patrols. In 1945, at the end of World War II, these patrols were immediately discontinued and the remote structures were abandoned. They were fair game for fisherman and campers and their use was on a first-come, first-served basis. Many happy and successful camping and fishing trips were made through the use of these facilities.

When my companions and I departed Sam's house on that inauspicious August afternoon, our destination was the abandoned Coast Guard cabin on the north end of Pritchards Island. At the time of our departure, we were aware that there was a tropical storm off the east coast of Florida which was stationary and had winds in the center of approximately fifty miles per hour. When we reached Pritchards Island at the point where Skull Creek empties into the Atlantic, we found the beckoning cabin vacant and not a breath of air stirring to give warning to the forces of nature which would be unleashed upon us within twelve hours. We relieved the boat of its burden of our camping equipment which we neatly stored in appropriate locations in the cabin. In those days it was unbelievable the quantity of equipment transported in order to make our stay comfortable. Food, water, ice, bedding, a stove, cooking utensils, and lanterns were the order of the day. A large waterproof canvas tarpaulin was carried along to protect these items while in the open *bateau*. Passengers also received the comfort of the tarp when the weather became unruly.

After unloading the boat and storing our equipment, we made preparations for catching our evening meal, having arrived at about four o'clock. Our plan for this day was to take the big *bateau* out through Skull Inlet into the Atlantic beyond and drag a small Otter trawl net for shrimp. Lying across the entrance to Skull Creek is a submerged sandbar which runs parallel to the beach. This is not unlike the entrance to Fripp Inlet, approximately four miles to the north. When we approached this bar from the northern and relatively calm inlet side, a most unusual sight greeted us. Even though there was not a breath of air stirring, there was tremendous surf running. This surf consisted of "ground" swells estimated to rise to six feet in height as they approached the shallow depth of the submerged sandbar just before they broke. These swells were about thirty yards apart from each other, and the largest ones were coming in sets of three, or triplets, as they are called. We pounded our way across these large waves with the boat taking a terrific beating as it came out of each wave and smacked the water below. The carpenter who assembled Sam's house was also the one who had built his *bateau*, and consequently it was very strongly reinforced. Once clear of these large breaking waves, it was smooth sailing, so to speak. We set our net overboard and the next hour was consumed in dragging it along the bottom for shrimp. My mind was also consumed with the fact that the heavy ground swells we had encountered originated from the storm located several hundred miles to the south. On occasion I shot a worried glance at the waves breaking over the bar at the entrance to Skull Inlet and wondered to myself what the trip back across would be like running with the waves. After about an hour of dragging the net, we pulled it in and examined our catch. Among an assortment of various species of small fishes, we were able to separate about two quarts of large brown shrimp, or "brownies," as they are called locally. This was more than enough for three hungry men, so I proceeded slowly back to the entrance to Skull which was about one-quarter mile away.

We were running parallel to the Pritchards Island beach, and as we approached the point I selected for crossing the entrance position, I moved the throttle up to half-speed and made a left turn. We were heading across the bar. In an instant the boat was being approached from the stern by the third wave in a triplet, and for the next twenty seconds or so the three of us received the most exhilarating and fearful ride of our young lives. As this large wave approached our rear, the boat rose upward, and when it was at the crest of the wave, I threw the throttle wide open. Sam's featherweight *bateau* shot forward, and we came down the steep incline of the wave at a fearful speed. We were literally riding a surfboard down a very large wave, our speed being greatly increased by that powerful outboard. Now, Heyward Jenkins and Christie Cummings were not what you would call avid sportsmen or fishermen. In fact this trip was the first time I was ever in a boat with either of them. They were both sitting on the middle seat of the *bateau* holding on the gunwale for dear life. Their greatest fear was that when we reached the bottom of the wave, the bow of the boat would go under. When the *bateau* reached the bottom of the wave, the engine was still at full throttle, and we shot across the bar like a rocket doing all of about twenty-five miles per hour. In an instant we were in the calm water on the back side of the bar. As I throttled the engine back to about half speed, I could detect a look of great relief on my companions' faces, and I knew that they were both thinking that I was a very skillful boat operator. In reality I was probably more relieved than they were, and there was no skill involved. Hitting that wave at the right instant was purely by chance. Bumping the throttle wide open at the precise moment, well, that's a different matter. We continued on to our camp where we enjoyed a wonderful supper of shrimp and grits.

We turned in early, but were rudely awakened at about 2 A.M. by windows banging and by wind-driven rain hitting our faces. I knew the boat was in a safe location in a nearby creek, and we had taken the precaution of removing the outboard motor and bringing it into the cabin—another one of Sam's rules. By daylight the wind had shifted around to the northeast and was coming in gusts of about thirty-five miles per hour. I knew we were in for some serious weather. Unbeknown to us the tropical storm off Florida had turned into a minimal hurricane and was moving north at about fifteen miles per hour. We were in the worst possible quadrant of the storm, and by 10 A.M. we estimated the wind speed in the strongest gusts in excess of fifty miles per hour. By noon, as we determined later, the wind velocity had reached minimal hurricane strength—seventy-six miles per hour—and it continued at this strength for another hour. Then, miraculously, at about 1 P.M., as if it had been turned off by a giant hand, the wind speed dropped to zero. The drenching rain stopped and the sun came out. We did not realize it at the time, but we were directly in the eye of the storm. It was at this time that I made a grievous error in judgement. This was 1947 and I, as well as the others, were totally unaware of the make-up of a tropical storm. In other words, we were unfamiliar with the storm's eye, and I made the decision to go home. The storm appeared to be over, and due to the immense volume of rain that had fallen, fishing would be out of the question anyway.

We hurriedly bailed out our boat and loaded our gear for the return trip home. When everything was securely covered with the tarpaulin, I started the engine and headed out into Skull Creek. All went well for about 500 yards. Then the sun became hidden by dark, forbidding clouds. In less than a minute it was as if all the forces of the universe had been loosed upon us. In an instant, wind gusts of seventy-five miles per hour were pounding us and the rain came down in horizontal torrents. I thought, but only briefly, about returning to the cabin. The engine was purring like a kitten, manfully doing its job, and was also protected from the attacking elements by Sam's great tarpaulin. We were carrying a very low profile so I headed for home which was an hour-and-a-half trip if there were no problems. In two miles we were halfway through Skull Creek, and due to the abnormally high tide, I took a shortcut which took us directly into Story River. When we came into Story River, I needed to make a ninety-degree turn to the right and proceed for about a mile to where I would take another shortcut that would take us in a straight course to our house. The wind was coming straight down Story River with its greatest force, hitting us broadside, and the motor did not have sufficient power to get us turned into the wind. In less than a minute we had crossed Story River and were about to enter the Spartina marsh grass. Seeing that the force of the wind would not permit a right turn and with the opposite riverside fast approaching, I turned the boat sharply to the left using the wind to turn the bow around. This maneuver enabled us to bring the bow into the wind, and once this was accomplished the motor was able to keep it there and we continued our wet journey. We proceeded directly into the wind and rain and when we reached the point for making the turn into our next shortcut, the Johnson outboard began missing on one piston. It was getting wet from all the rain and I knew that if one piston cut out on us, the remaining piston would not drive the boat under the conditions we were experiencing. I made a quick decision and headed for Sam's duck-hunting cabin on Old Island, a distance one-fourth a mile away. In a few minutes, running on one-and-a-half cylinders, we limped into the cove where Sam's tiny cabin was located. Once into this cove we were almost completely out of the storm, protected by a thick forest and high earth embankment. My two friends were totally unaware of where we were and of the presence of such a fine cabin. We remained here until the following morning. During the night the storm had proceeded up the east coast of the United States, and a glorious day with brilliant sunshine greeted us.

Two hours later we arrived at Sam's house where my parents warmly received us. We were alive and well and they were relieved. Sam's boat and motor were in excellent condition. I thought it wise to let several years slip by before I gave them the real story of what took place on this trip. If I had come out with the truth immediately, I would have waited a long time before being permitted the use of the big cypress *bateau* and Johnson outboard again.

During both of our harrowing experiences on this trip, my greatest fear was for Christie. Christie Cummings was an invalid and was on crutches most of his entire life. He could not swim a lick. In the event that the boat had capsized, saving Christie would have been my responsibility. Fortunately, this was not necessary. He passed away many years ago. Heyward Jenkins passed away in Beaufort in 1998. He was seventy-nine years old and pursued his profession as a registered civil engineer until his death. For the past fifty years, when I would see Heyward on occasion, I would tell him that his handprints were still embedded in the gunwales of Sam's *bateau*. I wonder why he never asked me to take him "down the river" again.

That Scottish Blood

Most of the blood that coursed through Sam's body was unquestionably of Scottish origin and this was displayed in many ways throughout his life. It did not go unnoticed by his friends with whom he regularly played poker on Saturday nights. There were always seven or eight participants and the site of this weekly event was at the same locale where the John Cross Tavern is currently located in downtown Beaufort. Even the game they played was of a single mind. Every hand was five-card stud poker. For those who are unfamiliar with this game, each player receives five cards with the first round being dealt face down and becoming your "hole" card. All other rounds up to and including the fifth round, the cards are all dealt face up. Thus, the "hole" card and its value are the key to the game. Its value can also be enhanced by the player's ability to bluff or to try to convince the others in the game that his "hole" card is of greater value than it really is. There was a monetary limit to this game, which these men would not exceed, probably due more to the economy of the times than from any other factor. The limit of the game was fifty cents per bet with a maximum of three raises per round. Betting began after the second round of cards was dealt. When Sam made a bet, the blood pressure of the other players always jumped a notch or two. Neils Christensen, who was one of the regular participants, contributed the rest of this story.

The time of this particular event was during the early 1940s. Neils said that during one hand, after four rounds of cards had been dealt, he had three deuces showing—Sam had a pair of jacks. Neils's "hole" card was the fourth deuce. Neils was dealing the cards and the "pot" had increased in size to a mighty ten dollars or so. When the fifth and final card was dealt, Sam's hand (showing) was improved by the addition of a third jack and he, being the first to bet, without hesitation, threw in fifty cents—the maximum bet permitted. All of the players, including Neils, immediately folded their cards, not wishing to contest Sam. When Sam exposed his "hole" card, it was the fourth jack. Sam knew when to hold; Neils knew when to fold.

Doctor Buzzard

Doctor Buzzard's real name was Stephen Robinson, although he was called "Stepney" or "Doctor Buzzard." Doctor Buzzard was probably the most renowned root or witch doctor of his period residing in the United States. He lived in the Oaks Plantation section on St. Helena Island and his fame was such that in a year's time, automobiles bearing license tags from all of the lower forty-eight states would enter his driveway. These would be people seeking a root or potion with which to put a hex on someone with whom they had a conflict. Consequently, he received a lot of mail, and, according to Sam, made a daily personal visit to the post office at Frogmore. Sam said many of his letters contained remuneration for services performed. As Dr. Buzzard opened each letter, he would examine its contents carefully. Most contained cash which he would quickly stuff into the pocket of his coat. The letters containing personal checks or money orders he would tear in half and deposit them in the trash can. Stepney Robinson was not a fool, and he left no paper trail that could lead an I.R.S. agent to his door. Doctor Buzzard was born in 1860 and died in 1947. Doctor Buzzard was buried in an extremely remote location on St. Helena Island, probably for practical reasons.

chapter 12
winding down

Sam and Nancy lived in their wonderful home and locale for forty years. In 1961, on his seventy-fifth birthday, Sam had a very severe heart attack. We rushed him into the hospital in Beaufort, and two days later he was transferred to the cardiac unit at the Medical University in Charleston. The day after his arrival there, the head heart specialist at MUSC, Dr. Boone, called my mother and me out into the hallway outside Sam's room to alert us to the fact that he would not survive beyond the next three days. Sam lived nineteen more years, outliving Dr. Boone. He died on June 15, 1981 at age ninety-five years and six months. Nancy followed him six years later at age ninety-one.

To Beaufort

Following the near fatal heart attack in 1961, Sam and Nancy decided to move into Beaufort. They bought a comfortable house on the Intracoastal Waterway adjacent to the Beaufort Memorial Hospital where they had many more wonderful years together. Their mailing address remained at Frogmore, and this was their excuse for a daily trip to their beloved St. Helena. And they did not want for anything. In 1958, Sam's brother William died in Columbia, South Carolina, leaving Sam $50,000. Now, that money meant nothing to Sam. He and Nancy were comfortable without it, and besides, he didn't know what to do with it. He consulted Buddie Glenn, and Buddie suggested he send it to his brother-in-law Harry Lightsey in Columbia. He told Sam that Harry would know what to do with it. Now, Harry Lightsey knew all the ramifications of the stock market, and he made his own decisions on how to invest Sam's money. By the time Sam died in 1981, Harry Lightsey had run that $50,000 to $400,000.

The Waterfront Park

Age did not diminish Sam's love for a practical joke. During the construction of the Henry C. Chambers Waterfront Park in downtown Beaufort, Sam and Nancy would make a daily visit to sip on a coke and to "sidewalk superintend." Sam and Nancy became very close friends with the job superintendent and several of his foremen and they looked forward each day to my parents' visit. One day, without warning, Sam and Nancy took off on a two-week trip. The day after returning home they went down to the Waterfront for a visit with the superintendent and his cronies. Sam had his story ready. The superintendent and his gang gathered around expressing how glad they were to see them safe. He said, "Sam, you were gone so long we thought some tragedy had come your way."

Sam replied, "No, nothing like that. I had a little problem over near the Gulf Coast of Louisiana that I had to go straighten out."

The superintendent asked, "What kind of problem, Sam?"

With a poker face, Sam said, "Several years ago I picked up an option on 500 acres of land adjacent to one of my oil fields that I thought had potential. One of my crews had been drilling for about three weeks with very little to show for it so I thought I would go down and see what the problem was. My geologists' tests were all positive for finding oil. I had my superintendent go another hundred feet deeper and he struck oil three days after I got there." These men walked away shaking their heads wondering who was this old man with the three-year-old Ford Fairmont?

Driver's License

On Sam's birthday in 1980, he turned ninety-four years old and it was necessary for him to renew his driver's license. Nancy went with him to the Highway Patrol office for this event. Everything went well with the exam until the young patrolman happened to notice Sam's age. He immediately became skeptical and was about to turn down Sam's request for renewal on the basis of age. Nancy spoke up and said "Young man, you must take into consideration the fact that he never drives unless I am with him and, therefore, there are four eyes looking at the road, not two." Sam got his license renewed.

Incredible Aim

In the fall of 1976, when Sam was ninety years old, my brother Edward was here on a visit from his home in California and was staying with Sam and Nancy. At noon one day the heating oil deliveryman had arrived, and Edward was outside talking to the driver while the underground tank was being filled. At this same time, two young ladies from the First Presbyterian Church arrived with my parents' daily delivery of Meals on Wheels. For the next five minutes or so Edward became engaged in conversation with the two ladies, telling them who he was, discussing Sam and Nancy, and so on. I was also present, and when the two ladies departed, Edward walked in with the meals and told me, "That gal Barbara is something else. She told me what a vigorous personality Sam was and that at age ninety he still liked to pinch." And the other lady added, "Yes, and his aim is amazingly accurate!"

Fix De Heat

During the last four months of Sam's life, his back had deteriorated to the point where he required constant help. It was necessary to maintain around-the-clock nurse's aides to assist Nancy in caring for him. One night in April, 1981, just two months before Sam died, I was awakened by the sound of my telephone ringing. I looked at my watch—it was 2 A.M. and on the other end of the line was Mazie, the aide I had hired to do the night shift. I said "Mazie, dat you? Wa bin de trouble?"

Mazie responded, "Yo daddy bin de trouble. He say de house to cole."

Now, I knew what the trouble was and only lived a mile away, but before going out at 2 A.M. on a cool April morning, I thought I would give it one shot over the telephone. I said, "Mazie—you no wey dat termostat ting bin in de hallway?"

Mazie say, "Yes, Suh. I no wey he bin."

"Mazie," I said, "here wey I wan yo fo do—lissen clos now. Go to dat ting an tun um to de lef til yo see de numba sebinty cum skrate up on top." "Yes, Suh. I got um," Mazie said.

"Mazie," I said, "if you hab any trouble, call me bak."

In about fifteen minutes my phone rang again. It was Mazie and she sounded desperate. "Misto Pear. I sho ain no how fuh fix dis huh heat ting. He duz hab to much numbah on um."

I could hear a voice in the background over the telephone and I said, "Mazie, who dat bin fuh talk?"

Mazie said, "Dat bin yo daddy fuh talk."

I said, "Wa he say?"

She responded, "He say fuh yo fuh git yo ass roun huh an fix dis dam heet." End of conversation. I got up, dressed and beat it around to 123 South Ribaut Road.

Unusual Man

About three months after Sam's death, I approached Nancy about the need to place a marker on his grave. He was buried in the new cemetery at St. Helena Episcopal Church. She agreed it was time so I designed a military style headstone which met her approval. I knew she would not want something elaborate. Then we had to come up with an appropriate inscription. We decided on the usual: name, date of birth, date of death;

For the record

and then to remember this truly remarkable man, we added, "An unusual man. He had the good life." I made a copy of our sketch, giving the original to a local maker of gravestones, and placed the order. Several months later I received a call that the marker was finished and was in place. I met the owner of the company at the cemetery and as we stood looking at the marker, I quickly realized something was not right. The middle "u" in the word "unusual" was missing. The tombstone manufacturer could not believe it and was beside himself. After giving this situation a few moments' thought, I told the man we would leave it like it was manufactured. Even in death Sam was truly an unusual man.

chapter 13

st. helena at the crossroads

The tide has risen and fallen in the rivers, creeks, and marshes adjacent to St. Helena Island for countless centuries. St. Helena has seen the elimination of its native population by conquerors from Europe, namely the French, English, and Spanish. It has survived several hundred years in which thousands of human beings of one race were held in bondage by another. It survived war, subjugation to an invading army, loss by its occupants of all real and personal property, and the humiliation of carpetbag rule. With regularity, many powerful hurricanes have unleashed their fury on the shores of St. Helena. In the great hurricane of 1893 alone, over one thousand St. Helena Island residents lost their lives.

Of all of the tragic scenes that have been played on St. Helena Island over the past 400 years, however, the last act has yet to be completed. It has unfortunately had its beginning. It is described in a single word and has been creeping like a cancer over the land since the mid-1960s. Sadly, it is called development. Others see it as progress.

In his book *Gullah* which was published in 1940, Mason Crum, Professor of Religion at Duke University penned the following about the South Carolina Sea Islands:

"About these modest islands there is a serene beauty almost beyond description. One who visits them with a view to finding sophisticated pleasures or, indeed anything modern, meets nothing but disappointment. No signs of progress are evident. The islands are like lavender and old lace; and he who does not love old things and the mellowing processes of time should not visit them. The Carolina Sea Islands are backward looking; they have no interest in the future." What would Professor Crum think today if he were to view the devastation—progress—that is taking place on St. Helena Island?

In 1955, the population of St. Helena Island was approximately 5,000 black residents with a sprinkling of about seventy-five whites. Then in 1960, development began in earnest. It was at this time that my prediction was that by the year 2000, the black population of St. Helena would remain fairly constant, but the white population would be equal to or exceed the black population. My prediction is right on target. The reasons for this invasion of whites are many. The construction of the Marine Corps Air Station in the late 1950s was one of the culprits. Many Marines at this facility and at adjacent Parris Island, finding Beaufort their last duty station prior to retirement, remained after retirement to take advantage of the many facilities available to them. Who could blame them? Included in the list of enticements were the use of the clubs and commissaries on the military establishments. Heading the list, however, were the free medical services provided at the nearby U.S. Naval Hospital. Other inducements for retirement in this area were the Technical College of the Low Country and the University of South Carolina where schooling was available under the G.I. Bill of Rights. Last, but not least, are free burial services provided by the U.S. National Cemetery, one of only two in South Carolina.

Military retirees are but a relatively small percentage of the overall enormous population growth in this area. Snowbirds, as they are called locally, or northerners seeking refuge from cold temperatures "up north," comprise a large percentage of new homeowners. So many have come, in fact, that it has been said that Beaufort has been invaded twice by Yankees in 137 years. The second time they took it without firing a shot.

Not all is bad in this regard. I believe that the preponderant portion of these newcomers are industrious, God-fearing people and give back to the community by supporting our churches and our community service organizations. Who, for example, would perform the monthly roadside trash pick up from Frogmore to Beaufort were it not for the residents of Dataw Island—newcomers all. And they are certainly forking out a lot of cash in property taxes.

The development of nearby Hilton Head Island is a strong candidate for laurels in providing impetus to the development of Northern Beaufort County of which St. Helena Island is part. Tens of thousands of visitors come to Hilton Head each year, and it is only natural that many of these find their way to Beaufort. In my opinion, Hilton Head Island is a classic example of how development can totally destroy a beautiful, pristine island. I do not believe the men who were the original developers intended for Hilton Head to become the sprawling metropolis that it is today, but once development started not even they could stop or control it. Development quickly jumped across the Intracoastal Waterway and is spreading like wildfire. One developer alone has a residential community underway that will eventually contain 11,000 houses. Residential and commercial development in Beaufort County and in nearby Jasper County is akin to a steam locomotive running at full throttle with the engineer lying dead on the floor of a heart attack. It is just a matter of time until developers with the right money take aim on St. Helena. The county development planners are trying to hold down development, but I believe they are too little, too late. The black landowners on St. Helena, who are in the majority, are very reluctant to sell, but in the end, money will move the land. There are several very large tracts on St. Helena that are still being farmed primarily with tomatoes, but if these farmers ever have several bad years back-to-back, they too will begin to sell their property. There are already several medium- to large-sized housing projects on St. Helena Island in progress, and there are many more hidden away in developers' files waiting for the right time to strike. In addition to developers with their larger projects, there are already several thousand individuals on board who have managed to pry loose small chunks of land from the local citizenry. Of the several hundred attorneys who are also now part of the establishment, one who is a long-time friend admits to producing an average of 100 real estate closings per month.

It is extremely fortunate that most of the barrier islands in Beaufort County have been protected from the bulldozer and the dragline. These islands consist of Hunting Island (a State Park); Old Island (Nature Conservancy, donated by Hermann Blumenthal of Charlotte, North Carolina); Pritchards Island (University of South Carolina, donated by Philip Rhodes of Atlanta, Georgia); and St. Phillips Island (development rights donated to the Nature Conservancy by Ted Turner). It is such a beautiful sight to fly along the coastline of Georgia, just south of Hilton Head, from Savannah to St. Simons Island (a distance of fifty miles), and look at the unspoiled beauty of six islands which form a chain. These islands—Wassaw, Ossabaw, St. Catherines, Blackbeard, Sapelo, and Wolf—are all protected by one or more agencies, or by their owners, from being spoiled by development. And when you add in Cumberland Island further to the south, fully three-fourths of Georgia's coastline is under protection. The only visible structures seen on these islands are the caretaker's cottages.

Sam McGowan came to St. Helena Island during the best of times— the 1920s. Local duck hunting was of the finest available anywhere, and there was not a place in the United States that exceeded St. Helena Island's quail hunting. The wild duck and quail populations simply disappeared many years ago. Life ran at a slow and easy pace. The only action for our sheriff and his two deputies was an occasional Saturday night shooting or cutting scrape at one of several local "joints." It now takes 159 sheriff's deputies to control crime in Beaufort County. In 1979 and 1980, I was privileged to become a member of the Beaufort County

Grand Jury. After this two-year term I was convinced that if it were possible, every county voter should serve at least one year on the Grand Jury. It would be an eye-opener as to what is really happening due to "progress." In 1980, the Beaufort County Grand Jury conducted a study of crime in the county. Every criminal indictment processed in the court of Common Pleas, or "Big Court," as it was called, dating back to and including 1948, was examined. Of principal interest were the number of total indictments, types of crimes, and of greatest interest, the sentences handed down by the Circuit Court Judges. This study produced some startling results: for example, the total number of indictments in 1948 was approximately 150, while in 1980 it was 1,200. There were no crimes related to drugs in 1948 while in 1980 approximately half of the cases were drug-related. Also, in 1948, it only required two terms of criminal court to dispose of all the indictments. In 1980, it required six terms to accomplish all the work.

The study also brought out that the judges in the time frame of 1975–1980 were still handing down slap-on-the-wrist sentences for many crimes, particularly in DUI cases, as did the judges in the cases looked at in the 1948–1955 time frame. It was also determined in the study that many of the total number of criminal indictments in the county came from activity on Hilton Head. In 1997, there were 2,511 criminal indictments in Beaufort County.

There was no automobile traffic to speak of, and if you did pass an occasional car you would know the occupants. Now traffic on U.S. 21 from Beaufort across Lady's Island and St. Helena Island resembles that seen on Interstate 95.

Not even the U.S. Post Office at Frogmore, which bore this name for over 100 years, could retain its name. In a referendum a few years back, the name was changed officially to St. Helena Island Post Office. I'm sure the Gullah Mailman twitched in his grave.

For two hundred years the English, French, and Spanish tried their best to devastate and plunder this beautiful land. They hardly put a dent in it. We are not to worry. The developers are finishing the job for them.

about
the author

A few days before Pierre McGowan was scheduled to see the light of day for the first time, his father Sam took his wife to Beaufort via the ferry on Lady's Island since the wooden bridge was still under construction. Upon arrival in Beaufort, he borrowed a friend's car and took her to the Oglethorpe Hospital in Savannah, Georgia. Five days after her arrival, Pierre Noel McGowan was born. It was December 20, 1926, which was also his mother's birthday. Six days later, she, along with her newborn, boarded a small steamer in downtown Savannah for its weekly run to the "Yard Farm" dock at Frogmore on St. Helena Island. Mrs. McGowan liked to joke that Pierre, having his first boat ride when he was six days old, has been on the water ever since. How true.

Pierre was educated in the Beaufort schools, graduating from Beaufort High in 1943. He served a hitch in the United States Navy near the end of World War II. He graduated from The Citadel with a B.S. in Civil Engineering. He worked for the Dupont Company for three years during the construction of the atomic energy plant at Aiken, South Carolina. He then worked for the Navy Department for twenty-seven years as a Civil Engineer, retiring from this endeavor in 1982. Pierre then worked an additional ten years as project manager for a company engaged in airfield concrete pavement. For the past forty-five years he has been a member of the First Presbyterian Church in Beaufort, South Carolina, where he sings in the Chancel Choir and where he has served many terms as Elder. He has been happily married to his wife Faye for forty-nine years. They have four children. He and his wife live on an island on the southern edge of St. Helena where he is busily engaged in anything involving the water.

bibliography

Crum, Mason. *Gullah*. North Carolina: Duke University Press, 1940.

Leland, Jack. "A Fast Disappearing Lowcountry Dialect," *Charleston Evening Post*, August 8, 1974.

Rosengarten, Theodore. *Tombee*. New York: William Morrow and Co., Inc., 1986.

Rowland, Lawrence S., Alexander Moore, and George C. Rogers, Jr. *The History of Beaufort County, South Carolina, Volume 1, 1514–1861*. South Carolina: University of South Carolina Press, 1996.

Rutledge, Archibald. *An American Hunter*. New York: Frederick A. Stokes Company, 1937.

Von Kolnitz, Alfred "Fritz." *Cryin' in de Wilderness*. Charleston, South Carolina: Walker, Evans, and Cogswell, 1937.

artwork